Road Trip

Barbara Fleming

Copyright 2019
Barbara Fleming

Original cover art/design by Trish Murtha, Loveland, CO
Email: trishjourneys@gmail.com
Book design by R. Gary Raham, Wellington, CO
Email:rgaryraham@gmail.com

All rights reserved. No part of this book may be reproduced, stored in a retrieval system, or transmitted in any form or by any means, electronic, mechanical, photocopying, recording, or otherwise, without the prior written permission of the publisher.

Library of Congress Control Number: 2019951730
ISBN-13: 978-1-7326985-1-2
ISBN-10: 1-7326985-1-1

Wellington, CO 80549

www.penstemonpublications.com

Dedication

This book is dedicated to friendship.

Acknowledgements

Many thanks to Patrick Clements for helping me learn about the Model T; to Cheryl Ravenschlag and Sylvia Falconer for critiquing the manuscript painstakingly along the way; to the Friday Writers" Group for once again taking me into their fold, and to supportive friends who patiently listened to me talk about this book, which came to me from out of the blue and wouldn't let me stop until it was done.

About the Author

Barbara Fleming, a native of Fort Collins, Colorado, has written or co-written several books of local history and writes a weekly history column for the *Fort Collins Coloradoan* newspaper. She is a member of the century-old Pioneer Association and of the Fort Collins Historical Society. An avid reader, she lives in Fort Collins with her cat, Shadow. Visit her web page at www.authorbarbarafleming.com.

Road Trip

Prologue

"Let's go on a road trip," said Lois, swinging her arms about and almost knocking over a vase on the window sill. (Lois sometimes forgot how widely her arms could reach.)

Susan looked up from her book. "What?"

"I said, let's go on a road trip. What fun we can have!"

"In the flivver?" Susan answered, her voice squeaky with uncertainty. "You've got to be joking."

"Why? It runs, doesn't it? It might be a little battered, but I'm sure it would get us somewhere and back."

"Where?" Susan set her book aside, giving her roommate her full attention.

"Wherever we want to," replied Lois.

"What about our jobs?"

"You haven't take time off in years. Surely the library can do without you for a couple of weeks. You've never even taken a day off when you didn't feel up to snuff. And I have never had a vacation."

"Yes, but would you still have a job when we got back?" Susan looked anxious. She flipped her unruly auburn hair out of her eyes. "Would I?" The thought of being unemployed in the depths of the Great Depression was terrifying.

"I'm sure I would. After all, I'm the best sales girl they have. And anyway I work on commission, so they wouldn't be losing money with me gone. Just some sales As for you, considering what they pay you for all the work you do, I can't see how they could get anyone else as good as you are for the same salary."

"How can you be so sure? People with PhD's are bagging groceries or standing in bread lines."

"I'm not entirely sure, but I do know that this is a terrific chance to do something different, something adventurous, while we're still young and unencumbered. It's just practically fallen into our laps. What have we got to lose?"

"Just about everything."

"Even so, couldn't we take a chance see what happens?"

"Hmm," said Susan thoughtfully, a comment she made often when she didn't know quite what else to say. Taking her response as a "maybe" not a downright "no," Lois announced that she would look for some maps so they could decide where to go.

"How in the dickens would we pay for it?" Susan's brow was furrowed with worry, another look Lois frequently saw on her roommate's youthful-looking face.

"Don't worry about that; I have money stashed away. You can pay off your share when we get back. And we can camp out—borrow a tent from a guy I know, make up bed rolls, cook over a campfire. We don't have to spend money on hotels or anything."

"Hmmm," said Susan once more, her remark a bit more drawn out than the first reflective comment. Lois interpreted the reply as assent, and she immediately began making plans.

And that's how it began.

Chapter One—Mutt and Jeff

At almost six feet tall (five feet ten and three-quarter inches, to be precise), Lois Parker was often accused of looking down her nose at people. She couldn't really help it, since a good many people were shorter than she was. Statuesque (a word she distinctly preferred to other, more pejorative ones), she was by nature gregarious, cheerful and optimistic. She was good at her job, selling dresses at a large upscale department store in downtown Denver; even on commission, even in the bad economy, she made enough to live on.

Susan Mayfield, on the other hand, was diminutive (a word she much preferred to "short"), shy and quiet, a temperament perfectly suited to a librarian—which, indeed, she was. Different though they were, Lois and Susan were fast friends. In fact, they shared an apartment. They had met at the beginning of their freshman year in college when they discovered themselves accidental roommates. On the second day of a class they were taking together, Susan was asked by her professor to stay after class for a moment. She complied, only to hear him say that she was bound to get an A in his class (American history) provided she accommodated him—or a failing grade if she did not. What Susan did not know was that Lois, for reasons even she was never entirely sure of afterward (a "creepy feeling," she later described it) had lingered near the doorway, with the door slightly open. She heard the man proposition Susan and strode into the room. "Touch her and you'll never hear the end of it," Lois said.

"I'll report you to the president of the college. I'm sure she is not the first student you have propositioned, but I assure you she will be the last." Stunned and surprised, the professor, an older man with a shaggy beard and a prominent bump in front, stepped back away from her, speechless. Together, the young women left the room. Once past the door, Susan gratefully hugged her savior around the waist (the only part of her she could reach). "I didn't know what to say," Susan told Lois. "Should we report him?"

Lois shook her head. "I doubt they would listen, but what we can do is drop this class and find a different one. We can also warn everyone we know about him."

Thus was a lifelong friendship born. Roommates by assignment, they might well have gone their separate ways, but the incident bound them irrevocably together despite their differences in personality. Susan, physically strong though she was, was a timid soul and valued Lois's courage and openness. Lois, outgoing as she was, valued Susan's intelligence and inner strength. Each found in the other qualities lacking in themselves—a fruitful combination. Friends teasingly called them Mutt and Jeff, which was okay except Susan was not at all plump, and Lois was not a string bean (she was, in fact, quite well endowed).

Petite (five feet two and a quarter inches, to be precise) as she was, Susan was often thought to be much younger than her 32 years. Her auburn hair, with its golden highlights, snugged around her piquant face in a wavy bob needing no help to curl (except when it escaped and fell over her eyes). Her green eyes, fringed by dark lashes and light eyebrows, dominated her oval-shaped face with its soft cheeks, dimpled chin and rosebud mouth. Susan despaired of her nose, considering it too patrician, but in actuality it suited her face exactly. Except for the hair, she might have been mistaken for silent film star Mary Pickford. Her figure was compact and fitted her height perfectly. One might have thought her delicate, but she grew up on a farm so was anything but. She had pitched hay, milked cows, handled a horse-drawn plow, planted and harvested crops and drawn water from the pump outside the farm house even on days when cold kept the pump from moving easily. Underneath that small frame was an assortment of strong, firm muscles.

Lois envied her friend that feminine appearance. Her own solid figure was nicely arranged along her frame; she was not overweight but always thought herself so. Victorians might have labeled her buxom. Lois saw herself as tall and clumsy, with feet that were a little too large, legs that were far too thick, arms that were way too skinny and gangly. Nothing about her body pleased her. Her light brown hair gave her special grief, being hopelessly straight. For years she slept with rags in her hair in a vain attempt to achieve something other than stringy—until a model at the store showed her how to create soft waves. At a beauty salon, she watched the brown strands (quite an ordinary brown, no hope there either) fall to the floor and what remained being gently framed into an attractive bob around her face. Oh, that face—squarish, plain, no distinguishing features whatsoever. Her hazel eyes were quite ordinary, her brows she considered despairingly bushy. Her chin was prominent, her nose seemed to her rather crooked, and her mouth was colorless without lipstick. What she did not know about herself was that her eyes radiated kindness, her smile gave her face beauty, and her demeanor, while sometimes a little brash (she believed that others saw her so) was open and friendly. She did not need to have classic beauty; hers shone from inside out. But of course she did not see it that way.

She often berated herself for her clumsiness, then with a laugh blamed it on being left-handed ("My brothers used to call me Leftie Lois," she told Susan)—an inclination she determinedly clung to in spite of persistent attempts by teachers and others to correct her of that supposedly bad habit. Pencil removed from her left hand to her right, she promptly replaced it. She learned to make the well-entrenched Spenserian handwriting symbols as a right-handed person would and developed a legible style. But she came into the world left-handed and she would not allow anyone to force her to be otherwise. Susan, for one, never considered that Lois's being left-handed had anything to do with her occasional clumsiness (yes, she did have to admit that Lois could knock things about at times). Rather, she attributed it to her friend's tendency to act before she thought about what she was doing, reminding her of Jo in *Little Women*.

As they gradually came to know each other, Lois learned about Susan's beloved older brother, Richard, who died in the Great War, about her painfully arthritic mother who had been bedfast and died when Susan was 17, about her loving father, Clyde, and about Enrico, the Mexican itinerant who wandered onto their farm one day looking for work and never left. He knew more about growing things than anyone Susan had ever met, and he was one hundred percent hard-working and loyal. From him Susan picked up a fair command of Spanish, while he learned English from her.

Susan learned about Lois's two older brothers, who left home as soon as they could. One survived the War to End All Wars as an officer who never saw combat; the other didn't enlist because of periodic unexplained fainting spells (which mysteriously went away soon after Armistice Day). Both men had settled far away, one in California, the other in Boston, and neither kept in touch. Susan learned about Lois's mother, who existed in an alcoholic fog, only occasionally emerging to have a maternal moment, usually misguided, and about her father, who distanced himself from his wife as much as he could and spent the majority of his time at his club downtown. A mining engineer, he was, as Lois described him, "as loving as a dead trout." Until the mine played out, he managed a silver-mining company's main office in the heart of the city. Then he went into banking and had somehow avoided the disaster of October, 1929; his bank was still in business and doing well, Lois said.

Her father paid little or no attention to the only offspring of his who was still around. Lois theorized that his sons had so deeply disappointed him (though she had no idea why, perhaps because they had not joined him in the banking business) that he had lost all interest in parenting and she was, after all, only a girl, who would soon marry and have children as all girls did (or should, in his view).

His bellicose, chauvinistic attitude toward women had turned Lois into a flaming, vocal advocate for women's right to vote and to do what they wanted to with their lives. In her teens she had sometimes traveled to other states and joined suffrage marches, even getting arrested once, and she had rejoiced to the depths of her soul when the nationwide vote was granted at last, even though Colorado women had been able to vote since 1893. She was one of the first women in Denver to join the League of Women Voters. (Twelve years later, she still saw a very rocky path ahead; clearly, women had many battles yet to wage.)

The two friends held each other up through broken hearts, tough classes, a few escapades (Lois, not Susan) and a few more salacious professors (Susan, not Lois; one of the professors was a woman), and Susan found the nerve to rebuff the advances, thanks to Lois. By the same token, thanks to Susan Lois developed a love of reading, to which she had previously been indifferent.

At one point Susan, who was attending college on a scholarship, had pictured herself as a professor, snuggled in an ivory tower, but she talked herself out of it when she heard the siren call of the Dewey Decimal System. Lois, meanwhile, was imagining herself as a valiant nurse, saving lives right and left, until she discovered that studying nursing meant dealing with unsavory bodily fluids and poking people with needles. So much for that. Neither of them was interested in attaining an MRS degree while in college. Someday, sure, but not just yet. And when they did marry, they agreed, they would not ever be typical housewives tied to home and hearth.

Lois was wise in the ways of the world. During the Roaring Twenties, she had enjoyed a fling or two, but having flirted with nursing she knew how to protect herself and was assiduous in doing so. She talked with Susan about her adventures, but Susan was too timid (she called herself a coward) to experiment on her own. Susan did not roar at all during that halcyon time. Instead, she dove into library science and earned a master's degree, securing a library job upon graduation. In their mid-twenties, both employed, they decided to get an apartment together. Living in a rooming house near the library, Susan had been going back and forth to the farm when she could catch a ride, which was not that often, but she finally decided that Enrico and Papa were managing just fine without her. Enrico had recently taken a wife, Rosita, who cooked mouth-watering

Mexican food and cleaned the house, so Susan's presence was not really needed. Lois had been working at the department store and enjoying a lively social life, ostensibly living at home with her father but not there very often. From time to time, she spent the night elsewhere. After they joined forces, Susan never asked; Lois never told.

Even though she never touched a drop, having seen what liquor had done to her mother, Lois enjoyed going to speakeasies and being with the people who clustered there, amid cocktail glasses self-consciously held at just the right angle, a plume of smoke wafting thinly from an elongated cigarette holder or held casually between browned fingers, and casual, meaningless chitchat. (The smoking was the most difficult to put up with. She and Susan both loathed smoking, even though they were accustomed to being around smokers. Smokers had a distinct and unpleasant odor; Lois would not go out with a man who indulged in what they called "that filthy habit.") Thus the years passed, Lois reveling in her carefree youth, Susan burying herself in books. But time was passing, and they were no longer so young, nor so carefree. The weight of the Great Depression was heavy; both knew how favored they were to have jobs and a place to live. On the streets of Denver they saw homeless people shuffling along the sidewalks, empty eyes looking at nothing discernible, shoulders slumped in despair, in line for food. They were both grateful for their situations. So how in the world, mused Susan, dared they risk their great good fortune and abandon their jobs?

With the two friends in their early thirties, like their native land trying to make their way through a terrible national crisis, they found themselves a bit bemused and unsettled. They were nearly ready to marry, each conceded, if the right man would come along. So many men had been lost during the Great War; there was rather a shortage of eligible men in any case. But they had not given up hope. That goal, however, was still elusive. For the moment, in 1932, they spent their evenings going to movies when they could afford to (with the new talkies, it was quite exciting), getting crushes on movie stars, drinking cokes and eating popcorn, or listening to the radio.

They loved *The Ed Sullivan Show*, where they heard Jack Benny, who generated hearty laughs which the nation so sorely needed. On *The Guy Lombardo Show*, they heard George Burns and Gracie Allen, who were just as funny as Jack Benny. Radio, they concluded, was here to stay. Lois had recently acquired her radio from an admirer and was so glad she had it; it provided them hours of free entertainment. To their great delight, they also owned a phonograph—acquired, sadly, at an estate sale Susan happened upon one day. When once-wealthy people could no longer hang on, they sold whatever someone would buy for whatever they could get. It was a sobering sight, and at first Susan turned away, but then she saw the phonograph, offered $2, and lugged home her new acquisition (which came in a case, with a handle) along with a small collection of records. To their great delight, they discovered that they could borrow records from the library, adding to their musical enrichment.

Susan, of course, read a great deal. Lois liked a good mystery; Susan would bring home books for her from the library. Christie was a favorite with both of them. Susan liked contemporary authors like Scott Fitzgerald, too.

Sometimes, in the evening or on a weekend, Lois would go to her second job, one she kept secret from even her closest friend. For her, it was not anything to get excited about; she was, after all, a sophisticated woman, but she knew Susan would be shocked. So she explained that she was posing for a photographer friend who was trying to make it on his own. She was in fact posing, but actually for an artist friend who, awash with success after having sold a painting to a Denver millionaire for a lucrative fee, had started offering art classes and needed a model. A nude one, that is. Unabashed, Lois would disrobe and display her magnificent proportions. After the class, she would get dressed, collect a goodly amount of money for her work, and return home. Not trusting banks after so many dramatic closures (not even trusting her father's), she kept the money in a strong box hidden within a chiffarobe in her bedroom. The money was accumulating fairly rapidly. She wanted to use it for some kind of spree, something fun, but she hadn't yet decided what that would be. Whatever it was would of course include Susan. Then along came the flivver.

Early in March of that memorable year Susan's father, a robust, hearty bear of a man who farmed in Eastern Colorado, dropped dead of a heart attack. With no family but Susan left, she inherited the farm—not worth much in 1932—and the farm equipment, which included a faded-green flivver, a 1927 Model T Ford roadster pickup. Susan took a short leave of absence to deal with the farm and to bury her father, whom she had loved and admired immensely. Many men might have left Iris, her mother, when she became almost completely incapacitated, but Clyde stuck it out, doggedly plowing, planting, tending, harvesting every year throughout her illness and for years after her death. The last couple of years had been bad, what with the drought and an invasion of Mormon crickets, and after his death Susan discovered that Clyde had been seriously in debt to the bank.

Susan found a friend who could take her as far as five miles from the farm—an easy walk for her, even though it was crisply cold—and when she got there, she sorted out the remains of her parents' lives and sold everything she could. The bank took the farm, including the tractor, but the banker was not interested in the vehicle, so she salvaged it. The aged cow, no longer giving milk, went to a kindly neighbor who agreed to let old Bess die a natural death. The barn cat she left there; it seemed to fend for itself well enough, and the old family dog she gave to the same kindly neighbor. No sooner had she buried Clyde, though, than Shep gave up the ghost. Susan thought he might not have wanted to live without his master; she buried him on the farm. Enrico and Rosita found work at another nearby farm. Susan hated to see them go, but she knew she had no choice. She gave each of them a hearty hug, trying to stem the tears. Rosita in her turn gave Susan a burrito (for your trip home, she explained in her broken English) and a shiny red apple. Enrico gave her a burro he had carved from discarded wood. It was perfect in every detail. He'd once told her how burros like to sleep on the

Road Trip

roads in Mexico in winter—it was warmer on the pavement.

Heartsick, weary, she prepared to head back to Denver and the comfort of Lois (who was a great hugger, as Clyde had been) to pick up the pieces of her life. The trip home, however, was fraught with tension, because Susan had never driven the Model T. She knew how to drive—most women did, by then, and Richard had taught her on an Oldsmobile Clyde used to have—but she had not ever driven that vehicle, acquired from a bankrupt neighboring farmer, which mostly sat in the driveway except when Papa had to go to town for supplies. Susan stayed home at the farm when he went to town. So this was her first intimate contact with the contrary little truck.

She walked all around it. There were two brake lights, one of which appeared to have been affixed after the truck left the assembly line and was slightly askew, and two large headlamps in front, but no indication of how to turn them on or off. The bed of the truck was quite short; slats of unfinished wood on either side helped keep cargo in place. Luckily, the running boards were good and wide, making it possible for her to manage, in one energetic leap, to get onto the seat. Curiously, the driver's door handle was inside, so she had to scoot over from the passenger side to open it. The previous owner had purchased isinglass windows, which were rolled up and, she discovered, chose not to unroll, so they were not much use.

First of all, she was hard pressed to see over the steering wheel. Being short (sorry, Susan) complicated her task immeasurably. Finally she put a block of wood under her to provide a little height—but that made reaching the floor too difficult and was extremely uncomfortable. So she gave up on that idea and decided she would just have to hunch forward and do her best to see the road ahead. That decision made, she studied the vehicle to figure out the mechanisms she needed to use to get the thing going. (It did not come with instructions.) After some experimenting, she found the starter button on the floor by her right foot. Grateful for the device (she had worried about having to crank a handle to get it going), she then studied the situation.

In the driver's seat, she inspected the apparatuses that made the

11

vehicle work. Starting the truck—which took a serious effort on her part to push the button down hard enough—she tried out the various attachments that confronted her. What made it go forward? Ah—a little experimenting led to the discovery that the throttle was on the steering wheel. Well, that would get her going. There were three pedals on the floor; she discovered that each one had a different function. The one on the left changed the forward gears, one low, one higher, (though she was hard put to see what was different between them). The one in the middle engaged reverse gear after she had brought it down hard all the way to the floor. Alarmed because she could not see where the truck was heading when going backwards, she tried the one on the right, the only pedal left unexplained. Sure enough, the truck stopped, rather abruptly. So abruptly, in fact, that she was thrown slightly forward and hit her shoulders on the steering wheel. Steering, she soon found, was no easy task. The truck seemed to have a mind of its own. She had to tug hard to get it to go where she wanted it to. She had no idea where the gas tank was and hoped there would be enough to get her home; she had about 75 miles to go.

Nothing for it now but to head home. She thought she could do it. She had to do it. She would do it. So off she went.

The open cab (no windows, canvas hinged top) was freezing cold. It was March and had snowed recently, making the roads snow-packed, icy in places. Wind whipped through from side to side, sometimes bringing along little sprays of stinging snow to hit her in the face. The car's worn tires did not grip well; she found herself constantly steering to keep it on the road. Luckily there was not much traffic on either side of the road, so she did not alarm other drivers with her sometimes wildly careening vehicle. She wasn't at all sure what she would do when encountering another car. Slow down? Stop altogether and let it pass? Given her other concerns, she decided that one would wait until the situation arose. With the Depression, people weren't driving all that much—who could afford the gasoline?

She soon felt her fingers, despite being gloved, tingling with cold.

Susan, however, was nothing if not determined. No goldarned auto was going to get the best of her. As a child, she had worked and worked at it until she finally could milk old Bess, relieving Papa of that task. She got so she could pump water from the well in the front yard, slight though she was, and she eventually got the best of the cranky woodstove that gave off heat and cooked their food. Baking was a challenge, but she mastered it in time, never becoming a great baker but competent enough; the food she baked was certainly edible, even given that quirky oven. She was not one to give up readily; she would not let that ornery old oven defeat her either. That very stubbornness got her through the long days caring for Iris while going to school, studying at night by candlelight, cooking and cleaning and all the rest of it. She would not have gone away to college if Iris were still alive, but Susan's mother had lost interest in life when Susan was still in secondary school—probably, Susan always supposed, after learning of her son's death soon after he enlisted, shot by accident during a training exercise. Richard had been the light of her life, her pride and joy, the male child to carry on the family name and work the farm. When that dream died, so did his mother. Generous as he had always been, Papa gave Susan the small amount of life insurance money he had collected when his wife died so that his brilliant, well-spoken daughter could go to college. She then was able to secure a scholarship, thanks to the diligent teacher in her rural school, which paid her tuition. Papa's money allowed her to live on campus and buy books.

Now, struggling with a car as uncooperative as that wood stove, Susan gritted her teeth and carried on. She *would* get to Denver, one way or another. How often Richard had said to her, "You can do it, sis. Don't give up now." She certainly would not give up. Richard would be very disappointed in her if she did. Besides, what would happen to her if she did give up? She was alone in bad weather on a nearly deserted road. Her only choice was to keep going.

Heading out of the small town, she saw a gas station with a single pump, a bubble tank made of glass, and decided to stop, just in case. Papa had always shopped in the town, she recalled, and she remembered his saying that the station was the only one around for miles. Embarrassed at not knowing where the tank was, she pulled in and got out of the truck. Good thing she had, for when the attendant (rather grubby, with lank hair, bent, almost toothless and looking as old as the hills and conveying a defeated air) came out of the crumbling building to fill her tank, she discovered that it was under the seat. (Six cents a gallon seemed like a lot, but she needed the fuel.) Unasked, the attendant explained in his toneless voice that it had to be there in order for gravity to feed the fuel to the engine. Oh. She tried not to think about what would happen if the car were to be hit, or to hit something.

The windshield was another hazard. Hinged in the middle with two halves that faced outward when open, it did not seal tightly when closed. When it began to snow lightly, she had to operate the wiper with one hand and steer with the other. She debated stopping until the weather cleared, but the road was so desolate and isolated, the terrain so flat and open, that she feared falling asleep and freezing to death.

The road was narrow and rutted. Occasionally, another road intersected, but there were no signs to help drivers maneuver through the crossings, as Susan soon discovered, so when she came to an intersection she slowed to a crawl, peering anxiously in both directions, before continuing. Mile by mile, she crept along toward home.

Her journey seemed to go on forever, even though she knew the farm was less than 100 miles from Denver. She had no idea how fast she was going, but if she was going even twenty miles an hour, the trip would take more than five hours. Darkness was creeping. She had no notion how to turn on the headlights. She began to shiver with cold and fear; once again, Richard's deep voice filled her ear: "Almost there, sis. Hang on." So she kept going.

How she had loved him! Some big brothers were not nice to their little sisters, teasing or pestering them, but Richard was an ideal older brother. He protected her, he patiently taught her so many things, he praised her accomplishments and he forgave her flaws. She missed him down to the depths of her bones.

Road Trip

Not quite ready to take up arms again and with not many miles left to go (she thought), she stopped for a moment to summon up the courage and strength for what she was certain to be the last lap. She took a small notebook out of her handbag. (The notebook, which served as her journal, went everywhere with her). She needed a few moments to compose herself before bringing the truck home to Lois; writing had always calmed her. Penning a quick entry (actually with a pencil, but it doesn't really matter), before darkness took over completely, she expressed her relief and gratitude — not, however, giving herself the credit she well deserved for her grit and perseverance. Still chilled to the bone but considerably cheered, she headed for the apartment, thinking about a warming cup of hot chocolate, a loving hug from Lois, and her lovely, cozy home. With those thoughts to buoy her courage, she started up once again.

I don't care to ever drive that truck again. If it hadn't been for Richard, I would never have gotten this far. Dear Richard; how I miss him. I wonder what L will say when I tramp in, cold and cross…

Chapter Two—Love at First Sight

Heart pounding, breath coming fast, Susan clung to the steering wheel with both hands and hunched over to see the road. It had begun to snow harder, the flakes swirling around in a dizzying array. Close as she was to home it still seemed far away. Not one for prayers, she wished at that moment that she were a praying person. The truck shuddered and creaked, alarming her. Would she ever arrive?

Then she heard Richard's deep, rich voice once more, reminding her that she could do it. She let it wash over her like a warm shower. The bravery that had been seeping away down her spine came surging back. Dear Richard. She had kept his secret: He was in love with a boy he knew from secondary school. She was the only one who ever knew, and she would never tell. If he had come back from the war, he probably would have gotten married, worked the farm, had a family, just as he'd been destined to do. Richard was not one to let his family down and follow his own path. His secret was hers to keep. No one else would ever know, not even Lois. Thinking about him helped the last few miles pass a little faster. And it finally stopped snowing.

After what seemed to be hours but was surely no more than 15 minutes, she saw the lights of the city ahead. Breathing more easily, she slowed down even more, wanting to be sure she made it to their apartment on Downing Street safely even though she was creeping there almost inch by inch. Denver had not received any snow, so the streets were clear. She took a deep breath and cruised homeward feeling pretty proud of herself. She heard herself say aloud, "I did it, big brother. I didn't give up." Instead of alarming her, the "tickety-tickety" clicking of the engine sounded soothing, almost as if it were Richard talking to her. The truck was running, she was near home, and she was still in one piece, albeit shaking a bit and half frozen.

Never in her life had she been so relieved to get home. Their building was square and squatty, sitting on the ground like a giant toad, painted a ghastly green color with brown trim on the windows and doors. Their apartment was on the third floor, which meant a climb (no elevator; their rent was cheap), but when she got there and had parked the flivver she almost bounded up the three flights, so joyous and so grateful was she to have arrived safely (the Model T, too). She decided to leave the few things she had brought with her in the truck for now. Lois could help her with them in the morning. The truck was open, no way to lock anything, but she was too tired and worn out to care.

She had no sooner opened the door than Lois enveloped her in a bear hug, rocking back and forth and saying, "Boy, am I glad to see you."

Of course Lois had no way of knowing what was happening with Susan or when she would be back. Normally, it was Susan who worried, but when it came to her best friend Lois fretted rather a lot, quite a contradiction to her generally optimistic temperament. Susan was usually shy and diffident and lacked confidence except in her work. Ah, but it was clear that Susan had risen to the occasion this time—gotten to the farm, dealt with the details, and arrived safely home again. Evidently, Susan had more steel in her spine than Lois had been aware of until now.

When Lois had had her fill of mothering, they sat down and enjoyed a cup of hot coffee—not the cocoa that Susan had envisioned, but delicious and soothing nonetheless. Coffee was a luxury, one they only indulged in on special occasions. Susan had a pot that sat on the stove to make the brew, and they both learned to drink it black to save money for other necessities. At first, it tasted bitter and harsh to them, but they soon grew to enjoy it—partly, perhaps, because it was such a rare treat.

"Now tell me all about it," Lois said, leaning forward and resting her elbows on her knees.

"Papa was badly in debt," Susan began. "The bank took the farm. I kept a few things of Mama's, found homes for Bess and Shep, and sold everything else that I could to his neighbors. They were so kind; they don't have much money either, but they found a few dollars here and there to buy some dishes and linens. The furniture was too shabby to salvage so I just left it. The bank took all the farm equipment, but they didn't want the Model T, so I drove it home."

Lois leapt up from her seat. "You have a car? And it runs? Well, it must; it got you here. I didn't even think about how you got back home. Jumpin' Jehosephat, Susan, that's super! Let's take a road trip."

The conversation evolved as previously recorded and ended thusly:

Recovering her equilibrium, Susan said after a pause, "Are you crazy? We're in the middle of a depression. People don't just go places to have fun."

"Never been more sane," Lois replied. "The roads won't be crowded, supplies are cheap, we're young and strong. Why not go? Come on, Sue (Lois was the only person who called her that), it's time to live a little, before we get married and settled down and are old and gray in the blink of an eye." Lois strongly felt that a trip would take some of the gloom off the general air of malaise that hovered around their daily lives and would cheer them up. Susan equivocated once more but agreed to think it over.

First things first—there was no way to secure the truck, which Susan had parked at the curb in front of their house. Anyone could get in, jimmy the engine a little bit, start it up and drive off into the sunset. A dilemma—what should they do?

Lois knew a guy (of course she did) from her carefree days who was living in a makeshift apartment over a butcher shop that had closed, thanks to an agreement he had with the bank which now owned the building (of course it did) to live there for free in exchange for keeping an eye on the place. It had a large sliding door around in the back, once used for deliveries, and would be a perfect place for their new acquisition. Plus, it was not far from their domicile. Perfect solution. Agreeably, Guy (yes, his name really was Guy) said they could store it there and even had a friend drop him off so he could drive it to its new temporary home.

Until they hit the road...but they would worry about that later. Meanwhile, the little conveyance was safe and sound, with Guy to keep an eye on her.

Once she thought it through and got used to the idea (which took a week or so), Susan decided that she could work up the courage to ask for time off and that a road trip could indeed be fun. Neither of them had ever been anywhere beyond their home state. Growing up on the farm, Susan had lived in a small world. It was only thanks to that very persistent high school English teacher that she had applied to Colorado Women's College and received a scholarship. Denver overwhelmed her at first. She had never seen so many people, so many cars, so many stores where you could buy just about anything. At home, she might go days without seeing anyone but her father and Enrico, and the general store in the nearby small town carried only basic necessities and farm supplies. She had never heard so many different sounds as there were in a big city. At home, she was used to the chickens clucking and the cow mooing softly, and with night came a profound, encompassing silence, relieved only by the occasional hoot of an owl or howl of a coyote. In the city the noise never really stopped, day or night. Traffic hummed constantly, if less so at night; horns honked, people called to each other, doors slammed. It took time to be able to tune it all out and sleep.

After the insurance money ran out, she had worked at the college library part-time to earn money for food and lodging, and that's where she came upon the Dewey decimal system and fell in love.

Lois also came from a small town, but one very different from Susan's. She was born in Silverton when her father had managed the mine there. When he moved from the small mountain town to Denver she was happy to relocate, but she returned in the summers to work at the local diner, and at a dude ranch, where she cleaned the cowboys' quarters, did laundry, cooked and washed mounds of dishes, saving enough money to pay her way through college. She firmly believed nothing would stop her from doing what she wanted to do. Her dream? She wanted to design women's clothes. Her mother, Gloria, had given her a sketchbook for Christmas when she was seventeen, and in no time she had filled it with her imaginative drawings. Her parents were comfortably off and could have paid for her higher education, but her father did not approve of women going to college. He happily paid her brothers' tuitions to attend the University of Denver and then graduate school. One brother served in the war; the other, George, did not. After the war Stanley went to law school; George became a professor of economics in California. Lois had little to do with her brother Stanley, who had taken a position with a big law firm in Boston and seldom returned to Denver, or with George. So she, like Susan, no longer had family ties, her father having given up on her and his vision of her life—marriage, children—and her mother lost in a fog of booze most of the time.

When Gloria was sober she tried in her way to act as she supposed a mother should, but she didn't really know how. So what came out was generally critical and negative, not what a girl needed to hear from her mother. When Gloria was drunk, though, she went beyond negative to cruel, calling her daughter, variously, a giraffe, a cow, or an elephant, depending on the mood she was in. The gift of the sketchbook, Lois always supposed, was made in a misguided moment when Gloria had, for a short while, remembered that she was the mother of a daughter and attempted to do something normal mothers of daughters would do, usually far from reality. No wonder Lois left home as soon as she could. After graduating from secondary school she went back to the dude ranch to cook for the cowboys (she was quite experienced in the kitchen; the Parkers had a cook who was, to Lois's everlasting gratitude, very kind and maternal. Lois hung out with her frequently and learned as it were, by osmosis), then she returned to Denver to attend CWC and never looked back.

For Lois and the Model T, it was love at first sight. One look at the tired little truck and she fell head over heels. Regrettably, the vehicle did not at first return her affection, despite the hours Lois spent cleaning, scrubbing, polishing and generally sprucing up the old girl in any way she could. The truck had originally been green, with black fenders and running boards. The sheen had worn off the paint, so the green was somewhat faded and splotchy; the right front fender had a noticeable dent. Nonetheless, Lois was entranced. She had driven her father's sleek, low-slung Buick convertible, and that only once. In a rare brotherly moment (his mother's offspring, for certain) George had taught her to drive on an old Plymouth that belonged to one of her father's employees. When she first started driving the Model T, the truck had bucked and snorted and even quit on her a couple of times, right in the middle of the street.

The two had to take the measure of each other. The whole setup of the Model T was different from anything she had encountered before. Luckily she was a quick learner, so it did not take long for her to get the hang of changing gears, steering, and maneuvering around other cars. As for the truck, she (Lois dubbed her Theda, after the glamorous, mysterious silent-film star with the rather racy reputation, Theda Bara) gradually got accustomed to Lois's not-always-gentle handling and frequent use of derogatory words (not aimed at Theda, only at other drivers). Lois had, after all, worked on a dude ranch and seen the cowhands handling the horses with firmness and calm, so she was confident that Theda would respond to the same approach. Soon enough it worked; Theda became putty in Lois's hands.

Susan marveled at her friend's skill. Lois could turn the steering wheel with ease, manage the throttle deftly and efficiently, reach and manipulate the pedals, and even back up straight. Lois, of course, had no trouble seeing over the steering wheel either. So they agreed that Lois would do all the driving, which delighted her and brought Susan great peace of mind. She would take on the role of navigator; as a librarian, she was adept at interpreting documents, and she loved maps. Night after night, the two friends pored over maps and books for tourists, trying to decide where they would go. After all, the whole country was their oyster. And what a very big country it was.

They were curious about the new road, Route 66, the first highway that connected states to each other. Built in 1925, mostly paved, it had already become legendary and alluring to travelers. In 1918, Susan had learned, there were only 3,000 miles of paved roads in the whole country. But the automobile was becoming more and more affordable and ubiquitous, and roads were in terrible shape. New, better roads were urgently needed. Route 66 went all the way east to Chicago and all the way west to the California coast. It was a sight not to be missed, whichever way they went.

They soon ruled out going westward, toward California. Even though it was said to be the "land of milk and honey," they decided it would be more expensive to travel there, and the glamour of Hollywood did not appeal to either of them. George lived near there, somewhere, and might have been able to show them around, but to get there they would have to cross a desert reputed to be mostly uninhabited and very, very hot, unless they went north to San Francisco. But that would eliminate Route 66, on which they had quickly set their hearts.

Plus, Los Angeles, the western end point of US Highway 66, would be busy in June as people headed there for the 1932 Olympics at the end of July. The stream of people pouring westward might find temporary work, but it seemed to Lois and Susan that LA would be frenzied, not much fun, full of job seekers (which the two of them hoped they were not), Olympic planners, construction workers, and hangers-on; there were always plenty of those. Moreover Route 66, it was said, was awash with broken families driving barely functional vehicles, escaping the drought in Texas and Oklahoma and heading west in hopes of a better life. Lois and Susan did not want to be amidst that tragic caravan. That left north or south, if they gave up on Route 66, or east if they didn't.

Their own state boasted magnificent Rocky Mountain National Park, full of breathtaking mountain views and great hikes, but it was in their home state and the idea was to leave Colorado. Farther north lay Yellowstone National Park, a wondrous sight to see, it was said, and the forested lands in Idaho and Montana. To the south were

Oklahoma, Texas, Arkansas and other states. But the drought had hit Oklahoma and Texas hard—what was there to see? They considered the Deep South—Alabama, Mississippi, Louisiana, Georgia—and decided that the poverty known to be endemic in those states would completely depress them; segregation was abhorrent to them, and there was nothing they could do to alleviate any of those problems. Plus, it would be intolerably hot there in the spring or summer. That left east.

And what was east of Denver? St. Louis, Chicago, the Great Lakes and more. East it would be, then. In two weeks, they concluded that they could get as far as Chicago and back. Susan was excited to go to the renowned Chicago Public Library, built following the massive Chicago fire in 1871 and containing volumes donated by Queen Victoria, Alfred Lord Tennyson, John Ruskin and other eminent Brits. Lois wanted to see Lake Michigan, rumored to be a breathtaking sight almost as thrilling as an ocean. Perhaps they could even take a ride on that vast body of water. They would come and go before the Democratic Party's national convention at the end of June, so they would likely avoid the crowds of delegates, along with the curious who came to peep and stare. Unlike the Olympics, they did not think there would be frenzied weeks of preparation ahead of the event.

(They both knew it would be a momentous convention and a critically important election. Herbert Hoover had done nothing substantive to alleviate the misery of the Great Depression; voters were frustrated and disillusioned. Some were very angry, but most seemed to be in the darkest depths of despair. A new president might bring hope, if not renewed prosperity, and surely would at least try to mitigate the suffering poor. Susan and Lois had often talked about the apathy that had infected the nation like a plague. People behaved as if there were no hope, all was lost, and they could only wallow in despair and wait for somebody to do something to fix it.)

Despite the fact that Chicago had a seamy reputation, what with Al Capone and all that—it was well known that organized crime had a tight grip on the city—, they decided to go there and see what sights they could without putting themselves in danger. They'd been told to avoid certain parts of the city, and they could easily do that. After all, Denver also had its less attractive areas; they had always carefully skirted around them. And along the way, who knew what remarkable sights they might come across? They were up for an adventure, whatever that might entail. Chicago, they learned, had much to offer—along with the library and the lake there were the renowned art museum, some architectural marvels, and Navy Pier, plus some luxurious hotels. They would seek out the highlights while taking care to avoid difficulties, for they were young, spirited, confident, adventurous and strong.

The two friends talked and talked about the positive and negative possibilities of the trip they were planning, coming eventually to the conclusion that they were capable of handling imagined mishaps and were eager for new experiences. As Lois had said, they were looking forward to seeing new sights and learning more about their country, ripe for exploring the unknown, before settling down. Careful Susan would balance impulsive Lois's sometimes misguided choices; optimistic Lois would offset her sometimes Eeyore-like friend.

They were keenly aware, of course, that the country was deeply mired in a depression, with millions of men out of work, legions of hungry and homeless people lining up for handouts, factories shutting down, banks shuttered, and even the well-to-do cutting back on luxuries they were accustomed to. Lois did well to sell one dress a week and was grateful that the department store remained open. Susan's salary was minimal at best, with county tax revenue at an all-time low. The state of the country, though, became their main rationale for taking a road trip—with Lois's stash to finance the trip (how astonished Susan was when Lois told her about it!), they might boost the economy a little here and there. They would meet all kinds of people and enrich their life experience, and they would see new sights without a great deal of expense; prices for everything had dropped, so food and gasoline surely wouldn't cost much. It seemed to them a propitious time to have a great adventure. Both of them began to get excited about planning the excursion.

Road Trip

I can't believe that I've agreed to take a trip with L in that old truck! But after I thought about it I decided it could be great fun. Whatever L and I do together is fun; she is the best companion a person could have. She doesn't get angry or upset and is generally pretty cheerful, whereas I can get gloomy if I let myself think unhappy thoughts too much. L has a good head on her shoulders. Where I could get frightened or upset, she will stay calm and work the problem out. I trust her completely, and I know we'll have a grand adventure. It's about time I had some excitement in my life. Books are wonderful companions, but they can't take the place of real life.

Chapter Three—To Wear or Not to Wear

To save money, Lois had suggested camping instead of staying at motor hotels, which had sprung up around the country a decade or so ago. "A guy I know has a tent we can use," she told Susan. (Of course she did; of course he did.) "We'll make up bedrolls and cook over a fire. It will be a real adventure." A truth Susan could not deny, although part of her was a bit apprehensive about what that adventure might entail; adventures were not necessarily beneficial, considering what she had gone through to get the truck to Denver. Not a thought she expressed aloud, though. It would not do to dampen Lois's enthusiasm. Susan had not seen her so excited for years. And part of Susan was equally excited.

Now they had to bend their minds to keeping Theda and her contents secure on the trip. Morris, the man with the tent, offered them what seemed to be good advice: "Remove the distributor wire at night," he told them. "I can show you how to do it. These cars are made on an assembly line, and I worked for Henry Ford when I was younger. That wasn't my assembly piece, but I know how it was done." Good advice, they decided; Susan, handy with tools, could manage it quite nicely once Morris showed her how—though she needed a small step stool to reach into the engine.

Ah, but what about the things in the truck bed? Here again, Morris to the rescue: "Tie a tarp on top. Run rope through the grommets and make a heavy knot of the two ends once it's tied down." Susan, who'd been in Girl Scouts, knew of a very intricate knot that would be challenging to undo unless you knew exactly how. Even if you did, it would take time. Those seemed like good ideas, so that thorny problem was, apparently, solved. Even so, Lois planned to bring a baseball bat with her, secreted under her feet, just in case. It would be right by her side at night. They would have to buy a tarp, an unexpected expense, but Susan did have some sturdy rope among her possessions—brought, purely on impulse, from the farm. Lois would have to borrow the bat. That was fine; she knew a guy...

Some folks might call these two sprightly young women old maids (for they were well past 21), doomed to live a long, lonely life as spinsters. Undeniably, they were well beyond marriageable age; most of their college friends were wives and mothers and had been for some time. Not Susan and Lois. Nor did they view themselves as being on the shelf. Far from it. They just hadn't met Mr. Right yet.

As for romance, Lois had Mr. Right clearly in mind—she just had to find him. He would be tall, naturally, so she could look up to him, preferably handsome as well (but it wouldn't really matter if he were not, provided he had all the other qualities she desired). He would be adventurous, like her, and smart. He would treat her like an equal, not a servant, and he would be kind and generous. She didn't care if he was rich or poor, but it would be nice if he had a steady job. He would want to have children—two would be ideal, she thought, one of each—and would make a wonderful, loving father. But most important of all, he would accept her almost-sister, Susan, as part of the family. If the fates permitted, she and Susan would find their mates close enough to each other that they could raise their families together. He was out there somewhere; Lois was sure of it. The question was, where? She'd met many men and dated a few steadily for a while, but she'd never had that tingly feeling that she knew would tell her she'd met Mr. Right.

Susan, on the other hand, didn't have a vision of her ideal husband. She did want to find someone who loved books as much as she did and was willing and able to talk books with her. Tall or short, slim or stocky, handsome or plain, she didn't care. She was sure of only one thing—that she would know him when he appeared in her life. Only one other important thing mattered besides books—that he accept her almost-sister as part of her life, for the rest of their lives, without question. If she never found him, she was all right with that; she could live out her life without marriage and a family. But she couldn't live happily without Lois. If need be, she would be "Aunt Susan" to Lois's children, and that would be fine with her. Susan had no doubt that Lois would find a husband. Someone so beautiful (Susan considered her so, even if Lois did not), so vibrant and full of life, so optimistic, was bound to be matched up sooner or later. Petite as she was, Susan never considered herself anything but ordinary. But Lois! She could be on a magazine cover.

One of Susan's favorite books was *Anne of Green Gables*, in which Anne discovers kindred spirits, people with whom she shares an intangible, indefinable essence that defies definition but clearly signifies connection. The moment she and Lois met, the air vibrated with it. They both knew they would be lifelong friends. She had known it with her father and with Richard—though not, sadly with her mother. She had loved her mother, of course, but love and the invisible thread that binds people together were, she discovered, two different emotions. So when Mr. Right came along, if he did, she would know. She would feel it down to her very bones; it would shimmer between them.

Not a woman of the world, so to speak, Susan nonetheless knew enough about the facts of life to understand what married life entails (after all, she had grown up on a farm), and she was certain it would suit her well enough. But having remained virginal into her thirties, she thought she could manage just as well without that dimension in her life, ignorance being bliss in this case.

Bit by bit, they began assembling gear for the trip: the borrowed tent, the formed bedrolls, a camp stove and cooking pots and utensils, an axe for chopping fire wood (a new experience for Lois, not for Susan), matches, a sharp kitchen knife, a lantern. And more: Lois gathered together some tools in case of car trouble, not entirely sure what she would use them for but feeling reassured to have them along—a hammer, two screwdrivers, a wrench and a pair of pliers. Susan assembled tools for changing a tire, just in case... And she began gathering the books she would need to see her through the trip. Although her personal library was very small, she was able to purchase dime novels from time to time—better, she'd decided, than nothing to read at all—and she sometimes brought home library discards. Thus was she slowly building up her own library.

Food was essential; they stored tins of canned fruits and vegetables, bought several boxes of oatmeal, raisins, and crackers, and satisfied their mutual craving for sweets with boxes of cookies. Peanut butter was an absolute necessity, so they stocked up on that. Luckily, Lois had a small pocket knife which would do for opening cans, and Susan had a portable coffee pot which would work perfectly for their morning brew, for they considered coffee vital to their survival on the trip. It was expensive and would be used sparingly, just one cup apiece each every morning, but they both had it on their lists. Even though they rarely indulged in coffee at home, they agreed it was essential to this adventure.

Lois borrowed a large gasoline can for carrying extra fuel, stowed on the running board, and they rescued from the alley another large can which would hold water for the radiator. Just in case. Another, smaller container would hold drinking water. Then each of them started putting together their personal kits. Naturally, Lois's included makeup and face cream. Quite as naturally, Susan owned no makeup so she filled her kit with other essentials such as a pencil and her journal, for recording the trip.

Once all the equipment was assembled, they had a packing trial run to work out the kinks, a caution for which they were later grateful.

Eventually they could no longer evade the Big Question: What were they going to wear? Traveling as they planned to do, camping out, did not seem suited to dresses. Yet society dictated that women wear dresses. Susan pointed out that she had never worn dresses on the farm; instead, she wore overalls, much more practical for working around crops and animals.

"Woman aviators wear trousers," Lois commented.

"So do some motion picture stars," answered Susan. "Like Greta Garbo."

"And explorers," added Lois. "And pilots."

"Even race drivers," replied Susan gleefully. She was thrilled that they could find so much support for choosing to wear trousers on the trip. Why not be daring? Why not be brave? It was the modern age, after all. Women had the vote; woman were doing all kinds of things once the exclusive province of men—playing golf, for heaven's sake. Flying airplanes. Climbing mountains. Racing cars. Repairing cars. Knocking on the doors of medical and law schools. Who said women had to be confined to skirts and dresses? Not those two intrepid explorers. Trousers it would be, and convention be damned.

A slight drawback—neither of them owned any trousers besides Susan's well-worn overalls, which would be too warm, but she knew a library patron who was a whiz with a sewing machine and would be glad to make them each a pair. "Better make it two each," Lois advised. "Just in case."

"Just in case" became their motto for the road trip. Gradually, exponentially, their "just in case" list grew until they were certain they had covered every possible contingency. They each bought a pair of sturdy boots (useful if one of them had to walk for help), broad-brimmed straw hats to keep the sun off their faces, and spare unmentionables in case they could not find a way to do laundry. They pronounced themselves delighted with the sturdy cotton trousers the dressmaker created: dark brown, with deep pockets, buttons up the front and belt loops, they were perfect for the purpose. From Lois's department store they purchased (rather, Lois purchased at a discount) sensible men's buttoned shirts with pockets and long sleeves that could be rolled up. Daringly, they also bought Army surplus aviation jackets that had absolutely charmed them. Accustomed to hanging out in second-hand shops, Susan was an astute shopper, tickled pink when she found jackets that would fit. Lois brought out her precious Kodak camera (sent to her by her brother Stanley when she graduated from college, a surprise gift she had never expected and was very grateful for) and persuaded the downstairs neighbor, Miss T. Young, to take a picture of them in their travel outfits. She smiled as she snapped the picture. "You ladies look ready for adventure," she said. Perhaps there was a tinge of envy in her voice…

Road Trip

The Kodak Brownie would come with them, no question. The trip simply had to be recorded on film. But it would stay right there with them all the time, being too valuable to ever leave unattended.

Well, we are outfitted and ready to go. I am at once apprehensive and excited. But I have no doubt this little book will be full of rich and fascinating stories by the time we return. If only I didn't have to talk to The Boss about time off... but I need to 'screw my courage to the sticking point' and get it over with. L has no qualms whatsoever. I envy her confidence.

Chapter Four—Bearding the Lion

As June approached they pored over maps, eventually deciding on picking up Route 66 at Joplin, Missouri. This meant crossing eastern Colorado and southern Kansas, but that part of the trip was unavoidable. Not affected quite as severely as Oklahoma and Texas, that area might, they thought, be a little less bleak. And the roads they would follow, a labyrinth of country lanes and wider highways, were dotted with small towns where they could find food, gas and water, or so they hoped.

But as Susan had known it would, first came the time to tell their employers what they were planning to do—the moment she had dreaded with all her heart. They had to ask for time off.

Lois informed; Susan requested. Lois told the head clerk of the women's department that she would be gone for two weeks in June. "It won't cost you anything," she said, "because I work on commission."

"It certainly will. It will cost us all the sales you won't make while you are away," was the reply. (Behind her back, Lingerie and Hats and Gloves called the head clerk The Sergeant. Her dour expression and sharp tone perfectly fit the description.)

"I have not had a day off since I started working here six years ago," Lois informed her. "I'm due, and I am going."

Steely gaze met steely gaze for a long, chilling moment. Then The Sergeant looked away. "Oh, very well," she said. "Go. But you might not have a job when you get back."

"And you would miss out on all those sales. You know I am the best sales woman on the whole floor. I've heard you tell people that when you thought I was out of your hearing."

The reply was a muttered grunt, which Lois took as affirmative. No more was said on the subject.

For Susan, though, it was a different matter altogether. It took her three days to work up the fortitude to beard the lion, so to speak. Even getting so far as to knock on the library director's door took all her fortitude—much less going in and talking to him. Anyone who did not work there would think Horace Pendergrass a mild-mannered man, a small, insignificant personage in a big, not always friendly world. He was indeed small, only a few inches taller than Susan. He wore wire-rimmed glasses, perched inelegantly and slightly crookedly on his nose. He was always attired in some version of a tattered cardigan, striped shirt and baggy pants held up with suspenders and invariably a little too loose for his small frame. He favored black bow ties and combed his oiled hair straight back, no doubt to cover a burgeoning bald spot. Oddly, he sported a cigarette holder dangling from his lower lip although he had never been seen to smoke, there was no ashtray on his desk, and they all knew he would have been livid had he caught any one of his staff puffing on a cigarette.

Unlike outsiders, Susan knew what lurked underneath that placid exterior. Pendergrass could roar with the best of them. He was meticulous in his manner and extremely specific in his demands. The card catalogue must be maintained in a certain way, with daily reviews. He must approve every new card and determine that each catalogue entry was correct. Book purchases were scrutinized down to the penny even though there was a librarian in charge of buying books. Pendergrass insisted that the author be well known, the book not be obscene, and the price be his idea of reasonable. Rarely would he approve buying more than one copy of even the most sought-after books, the best sellers. As for his employees' behavior (all women, it should be noted), they must be morally impeccable and demure, lady-like, in appearance. He would tolerate no deviations—such as trousers.

Susan always dressed with great care when she went to work. He would never accept less than impeccable attire (half-calf length dresses, of course, in muted colors—she had three dresses, two

33

skirts and four blouses that she carefully rotated) and in fact he had been known to send employees home if he did not consider them suitably attired.

On the third day Susan finally overcame her timidity and knocked on The Boss's door. "Come in," said the stentorian voice behind the door—a surprisingly strong, deep voice for such a slight person. She opened it cautiously, peering around the door until she was finally inside his office (which, it must be said, was surprisingly neat and orderly given the man's personal appearance, not a pencil or scrap of paper out of place).

"I need to request some time off, sir," she said in a shaky voice. (Pendergrass insisted on being addressed as "sir," despite being a big fish in a very small pond.)

"Why?" he roared at her. "You just had time off when your father died! Four whole days. Wasn't that enough?"

"Personal reasons," she replied, gradually gaining confidence in the justifiable nature of her request. After all, she had not had time off in ten years except for Papa's death. She was due. She was overdue (so to speak).

She was standing; he was still sitting. She felt bravado seeping into her bones, from the toes on up. Then he stood up and came around his desk to glare at her.

"Which are?"

Susan cleared her throat. "Personal, sir, as I said. I will be gone for two weeks in June." She was not going to lie or make up a fake excuse, nor did she choose to divulge the reason. She stood her ground.

"Personal." He stood and thrust his hands into his pants pockets, which she thought made him look a little bit like a circus clown the way the pockets stuck out on each side of him. His lips moved the cigarette holder up and down. There was a long, painful silence.

"You do realize I cannot pay you when you do not work."

"Of course, sir." Lois had prepared her for that reaction, so she showed no surprise. "I do not expect to be paid when I am not here." Like all the other librarians, she was paid an hourly wage (a meager one at that, but just enough to sustain her). Of all the staff only The

Boss was paid a monthly salary, the amount of which was a carefully guarded secret. Unfair, her fellow librarians complained (behind his back, of course); he had no family to support—how could he, a man like that? And they'd never seen a wedding ring—and he probably still lived with his mother, though no one had ever discovered that he had one. He certainly did not need a guaranteed wage. But—he was a man. They were women. That was the way of things.

The Boss cleared his throat. "Very well," he said. "Just make sure you do not leave any tasks undone before you go." He had not promised that her job would still be there on her return, but she was counting on his penny-pinching nature to not spend time or money training a replacement. She chose not to ask. He turned away from her and bent over some papers on his desk.

Limp with relief, Susan nodded and walked out of the room, then promptly sank down into a chair. She felt a little giddy, truth be told, and her heart was pounding. It took her a few moments to regain her composure.

The last hurdle, then, had been scaled successfully. The trip was really, finally, going to happen. A friend of Lois's lent them a heavy canvas tarp to cover and secure their goods in the back of the pick-up, saving them that expense. Lois had indeed found a baseball bat to borrow, which was promptly ensconced in the cab of the truck. "Not that I'm expecting trouble," she told Susan, "but you know, just in case…" Susan was fine with that addition to their accoutrements. In fact, she tucked in her heavy, flat iron, knowing she would probably not be ironing but viewing it as a means of defense in the unlikely event that self-protection became necessary. The stark truth was that they were two women traveling alone. Cautious though they intended to be, it was wise to be prepared.

A slight hitch happened a few days before their departure date when the man who was storing Theda for them told Lois the tires on the truck were too far gone to be safe on such a trip. He didn't want her to go with those tires; they had to have new ones. Lois was taken aback; she didn't think her travel funds would cover such an expense. But then an incident happened that Lois, who was something of a mystic at times, declared was a sure sign that the trip was meant to happen: only a block or so away from the storage space where Theda was abiding, a 1926 Model T pickup was involved in a serious accident, run off the road by a large, unbalanced delivery truck which careened around a corner too fast. Remarkably, the driver was unhurt, having only some cuts and bruises, but the poor little truck was a goner, its chassis twisted beyond redemption, Morris told them. The owner was salvaging the body for parts and had a set of almost-new tires to sell for only $2 apiece. Lois was dismayed; that would dig deeply into her stash for the trip, but then Morris offered to loan them the money to purchase the tires and even to put them on Theda. Lois accepted the offer. They would repay Morris bit by bit when they returned.

"Why would he do such a nice thing for you?" Susan wondered.

Lois merely smiled enigmatically. "We're old friends," she said. "I've done some favors for him in the past." Susan decided not to pursue that conversation any further. So now Theda was all outfitted with practically new tires, which would make for a much safer trip.

Should these eager travelers have felt somewhat apprehensive? After all, they would be traveling during a time when the bottom had fallen out of the country. Might there be deprived people desperate enough to rob or attack them, or try to steal Theda? And what would most men think of them? Helpless females, unable to cope whenever something went wrong...

Perhaps they should have felt a bit anxious. But such thoughts did not cross their minds; they were too excited about what lay ahead. Neither ignorant nor naïve, they had prepared for the possibility of danger even though in their minds that seemed unlikely to happen, so they declined to worry. Their glasses were undeniably rose-colored.

Miss T. Young, who lived directly below them on the second floor and had never revealed her first name, generously agreed to collect their mail. Lois secreted their funds within the folds of her magnificent bosom. They packed their first-day picnic, donned their traveling outfits, locked the door behind them, and set off on their grand tour.

Road Trip

Here we are on the road at last! I find myself quite eager to see what lies ahead and ready to tackle whatever comes. With L by my side, we will tame the dragons, whoever and whatever they might be, and relish the joys which are sure to appear. Tally ho!

Chapter Five—On the Road at Last

"Did we forget anything?" Susan asked as they settled into the cab.

Lois, behind the wheel, shrugged. "If we did, I guess we didn't really need it. Come on, Theda, let's get this show on the road." She started the engine.

Theda responded promptly, taking them east out of the city with aplomb if not at racing speed. The sights they passed were not heartening—rundown row houses, empty shops with broken windows, stray dogs, long bread lines. (Again, the slouched posture, the air of hopelessness and defeat, permeated the air whenever they saw a bread line. Susan was struck by the attire of the men, who dressed as though they were on their way to work—dark pants, white shirts, ties and the inevitable fedoras. Many had cigarettes dangling from their lips. The few women in the lines chatted among themselves, but not the men.)

Soon enough they were in the country, really and truly on their way. The road was narrow and rutted, as Susan already knew, and signposts were few and far between. They went through several small towns, some of them showing signs of life, others seeming to be ghost towns. Susan recorded the name of each one in her journal. Just the sight of a deserted town made her thirsty. She took small, judicious sips from her canteen from time to time. The water was warm, not too thirst-quenching, but it was wet. It would do.

The countryside was dry and bleak, crops drooping in the blazing sun, little air stirring around to move the leaves. Trees were few and far between.

Road Trip

Getting to the Kansas border was challenging to say the least. Although most of the towns they went through were on Susan's map, often the roads were not; she drew them in as they rode along. Road signs were sparse, most of them indicating that another town was coming up, so they just kept heading east, asking for the best route whenever they stopped in a town. There was no direct route east; roads meandered from one spot on the map to the next, and clearly no single entity was responsible for keeping the roads passable. Most were deeply rutted, quite narrow, and pockmarked with little holes. Sometimes Lois would have to stop and remove an obstacle like a fair-sized branch or rock; sometimes, she just drove around it.

They came upon very little traffic going either direction; at times, Susan had the sensation of being on an alien planet amidst unknown terrain, nothing familiar except her companion and the little truck to orient her. Then they would chug into another little town, see people, and the feeling would dissipate.

The flivver's top speed seemed to be about forty or forty-five miles an hour, though they had no real way of knowing since nothing on the dash indicated speed and no speed limit signs appeared on roadsides. Lois guessed around forty based on how long it took to get from one landmark to the next. Once Lois braked suddenly so as not to hit a rabbit that was streaking across the road, a thin red fox close on its heels. Susan, the country girl, was accustomed to the ways of nature. Lois, the city girl, said she hoped the rabbit got away. "I could never run over an animal," she declared, "and I don't want to see one animal eat another one." Susan held her tongue. Like every other creature the fox had to eat to survive, after all.

They also had no way to tell how much gasoline they had, which made Lois nervous though she didn't say so. She stopped at the first town where she saw a gas pump and at every one they encountered the rest of the day. They quickly discovered that the radiator, exposed to the outside air, accumulated bugs that clogged it up, so every time they stopped Lois took a wire brush which she had fortuitously brought along "just in case" and cleaned it off.

Susan noticed that Lois bit her lip from time to time and wiggled around in her seat more than seemed normal as she drove. Lois was clearly on edge that first day, causing her to seem anxious, not her usual posture; Lois had always given the impression to Susan of being on top of whatever situation she found herself in. But they were determined to enjoy themselves, to have a wonderful time, so neither told the other how she was really feeling. Unlike Lois—and very unlike herself—Susan bubbled with excitement and talked more than she normally did (for she was capable of long stretches of complete silence, as Lois well knew). Lois, normally the talkative one, barely spoke.

For a time the road followed a river which, though low, was still flowing. Lois braked when they saw a magnificent bald eagle fly in front of them, dive into the water and come up with a small fish in its beak. "Too fast for a picture," she said. "Too bad." Once or twice, Lois stopped just to gaze at the endless blue sky, a view her city eyes were not used to since she had left her mountain hometown. The blue seemed more intense, deeper, than in the city; only a few fluffy clouds dotted the sky. Before, behind and beside them were flat plains, above them the cerulean expanse. Lois did come to a full stop after a time, got out her camera, and took a picture of the landscape to the east. They could still see the outline of mountains to the west, so she captured that on film too. Even though the photos were black and white, they would still be dramatic reminders of memorable scenery. Lois had heard murmurs about the possibility of color film from time to time, but she thought the reality was probably in the far distant future. She had an exceptional visual memory and the skill to color the photos later, which she planned to do.

They had not gone very far when the mountains behind them, the skyline they were so attuned to, faded from view. Everything around them, in every direction, was brown and flat.

They continued to encounter little traffic. None was going their way, but now and then a car or small truck heading west hugged the other side of the road. Once or twice Lois had to pull off to the shoulder to allow another vehicle room to get by. They spotted a four-legged creature scurrying across the road—another fox, Susan said, and she noted how beautiful it was. "They are the bane of a farmer's existence because they go after chickens, but I have always thought they were gorgeous." Sleek, red-coated, long-tailed, the fox bent low and streaked through the tall grass on some very important errand and was soon lost to their sight. Lois was tickled pink to have seen two foxes in the flesh; all she'd ever seen before was pictures of them. There weren't any in the zoo. (A good thing, too; the poor creatures would have been miserable being so confined, Susan thought.)

Map reading and locating the correct road was proving to be time-consuming for Susan. So intent was she on reading a map that she almost failed to notice nature's call, but soon it became impossible to ignore. She was embarrassed, even with Lois, but it had to be said. "Lois, dear, I..." Lois took a quick look at her passenger. "So do I," she replied. Thus began their first quest, amid companionable chuckles: to find a ladies' facility. They went through one more deserted town and then came to a roadside gasoline station, one pump in front of a small general store. "Surely..." Lois remarked. She pulled in beside the pump. A rather withered, elderly man wearing baggy overalls with deep front pockets came out. "Help you?" he said, eyes on the ground. Lois, the bold one, answered that they would like to fill the tank and please, could they use the ladies'?

"Don't have no ladies," was the reply. "Just one toilet (he pronounced it "terlet"). Round the back." He jerked his head toward the rear of the store. Susan leapt out as fast as she had ever moved and headed for the door she sought so eagerly. She emerged a few minutes later, grimacing, wiping her hands on her trousers, and nodded at Lois, who scooted around to the back of the store.

Not until they were back in the Ford did they talk about it. "Filthy," said Susan. "I didn't dare sit; I squatted." "Me too," replied her friend. "One soiled towel to wipe my hands with, cold water, no soap..." Then out pealed her hearty laugh. "Well, Sue, we wanted adventure, wanted to see the world—what a start, eh?" And they both laughed until they were out of breath.

"I'll be better prepared next time," Susan vowed once they were underway again. They had laid in a supply of hand towels; she would dig one out before venturing into unknown territory again. After relief came hunger. They passed one more small town before coming upon a pleasant, deserted roadside park, featuring shade provided by a single lonely, very tall tree with broad leaves, a picnic table and even a fire pit. Lunch was delicious—peanut butter sandwiches, carrot sticks and canned peaches, accompanied by iced tea. (Well, not so iced any more; even though they had put the bottle well out of the sun, it still got very warm.)

Refreshed, they set out again. Quest number two became a suitable place to camp for the night. The landscape had not changed; it was still flat and open with only a tree here and there, and camping in such circumstances was not particularly appealing. But they would have to pick a spot before it got dark.

"Are you getting tired?" Susan asked. "You've been driving a long time. This truck isn't that easy to handle."

"Theda? She's okay. Just needs a firm hand, like a horse."

"What about you, though?"

Lois leaned back against the seat. They had always been honest with each other. Pride and pettiness never came between them. "You're right," she conceded. "I am getting tired." She pulled off the road. The seats, she conceded, were uncomfortable, and the old thing bounced up and down quite a bit.

"But where in the world can we camp? I don't want to just be out in the open." Susan fell silent while she pondered. Then—"I've seen a few farms around here that might be occupied. What if we asked to camp on someone's farmland? We'd be off the main road, with a little protection from the elements, and not completely alone. Surely there are still a few working farms around here. Papa and I would let people do that sometimes."

"Great idea, friend." Lois pulled back onto the road and they began scanning the land to find a farm that looked likely. One of Susan's gifts was very sharp eyesight, so she was the lookout. After an hour or so she said, "Up there." Lois saw a two-story brick house perched on a hill, surrounded by tall trees in full leaf. A short distance away stood a large barn which had a gleaming coat of whitewash and a sturdy roof. No animals or people were visible, but the place did not look deserted either, for there was a tractor in a field that had not rusted away and in the distance she could see a flock of sheep.

"Off we go," Lois said cheerfully, and she headed the Ford toward a narrow trail that led to their goal. Getting there took a while, and all of her intense concentration, for the path was deeply rutted and in places seemed to disappear altogether. Theda bounced back and forth like a ship at sea. But they did arrive at the barn after about half an hour. Lois stopped the truck and got out. She walked over to the house and knocked on the door. After a tense few minutes, it swung open to reveal a substantial young woman of medium height wearing an apron and holding a small child by the hand.

"Hello," she said with a friendly smile. "And who are you?"

"My name is Lois Parker, and this is my friend, Susan Mayfield. We are on a road trip, looking for a place to camp. We wondered if you would mind letting us camp overnight on your land."

"Land sakes," said the young woman, "I thought you might be looking for a handout. People come by now and then asking for food or water, or some milk for a young'un."

Susan spoke up then. "We only want a place to set up our camp," she said, surprising herself at how forward she was getting. "We won't bother you."

The woman, who introduced herself as Mary Jane Batson, gestured. "You ain't a bother. Come on in and set a spell," she said. "Get outta the sun." She led them to her parlor, obviously seldom used, and invited them to sit. "I'll get some ice tea," she said. "Judy, you come along with me." The child, who looked to be six or seven, turned her wide-eyed gaze away from the young women, stuck her thumb in her mouth, and followed her mother to the kitchen. She said not a word.

After a few minutes Mary Jane, with Judy at her heels, returned with a tray that held not only iced tea but homemade sugar cookies which made their mouths water. She sat down on the sofa. "Now then, what in tarnation gave you the notion to go on a road trip in times like these?"

"Susan inherited that truck out there and we just decided to go on a trip," said Lois. "I know it looks crazy, with the country in such a fix, but we thought we should do it while we're still young and single. I had some money put by and we just said, 'Why not?' So here we are."

Mary Jane took all that in with a growing smile. "You girls have got some gumption; I'll say that for you. The two of you alone, no man, headin' out to lord knows where—I am mighty impressed." She leaned back against the chair. "Now then, there'll be no nonsense about camping out. My Ted and I have a spare room, and you can spend the night. He'll be in from the field pretty soon, we'll have a bite to eat, and then off to bed you go."

"Oh," said Lois, "we couldn't impose like that."

"Who said you was imposin'? Know how long it's been since I had another woman to talk to? My goodness, you two are a sight for sore eyes."

There seemed to be no alternative but to accept such a tempting, gracious offer, so they did. In due time My Ted, a big, friendly man who reminded Susan achingly of her father, came in from the fields, washed up and sat down to enjoy the delicious repast Mary Jane set before them. They had chicken stew with potatoes and carrots, homemade yeast rolls, and sweet potato pie for dessert. My Ted bowed his head and said grace before digging into the food, for which he thanked both the lord and his good wife. Young Judy ate as heartily as everyone else but said not a word during the meal and soon was whisked off to be bathed and tucked in. Mary Jane came back down a short while later, refused offers of help to clean up the kitchen, and sat down to talk with them even after her husband had gone to bed. She wanted to know about the big city where Lois and Susan lived, about the latest fashions, about their jobs. She wanted to know everything they could tell her.

Finally, seeing how exhausted her guests were, she headed toward the stairs. Lois, the motherless child, looked at Mary Jane's ample bosom and thought how wonderful it would be to rest her head on that maternal shoulder. Mary Jane turned and, seeing the longing in Lois's eyes, held out her arms. Lois bent into the hug and thought she would never forget that moment. Should she ever have children, she vowed, she would hug them every day. Then Susan, the reticent introvert, moved into Mary Jane's embrace as soon as Lois stepped away. The warm hug brought tears to her eyes, reminding her of Clyde's loving, frequent bear hugs and bringing a pang of grief. How she missed him!

Mary Jane led the way upstairs and showed them to the spare bedroom. She bade them goodnight. Though the house had no electricity (they had a kerosene lantern to light the room), it did have modern plumbing, for which they were grateful. Both of them relished the clean bathroom, the fresh towels Mary Jane set out, and the fragrant soap, obviously handmade, that smelled of lavender. The double bed was covered with a beautiful quilt, intricately designed with varieties of colorful flowers. The linen smelled sweet and fresh. A crocheted antimacassar covered the arm chair.

"We have landed in heaven," Lois pronounced. "This woman is amazing. So talented! So kind." Susan nodded her agreement, too weary to say a single word, and climbed gratefully into bed. Before long both were dead to the world, Susan clinging to the edge of the bed while Lois sprawled all over the middle. But Susan did not mind. She was as happy as she could remember being since her father died. To be cared for in such a generous fashion, to be welcomed so warmly, was much more than they could have dreamt would happen. This certainly was an auspicious beginning.

We spent last night in the lap of luxury instead of out among the stars, and I for one am glad of it. Even though Lois took up most of the bed, I slept well enough and am ready for more adventure. What nice people the Batsons are. I have always believed the world is full of more good people than bad ones; this proves my case. Onward and upward we go!

Chapter Six—Day Two and Beyond

After profusely thanking their hosts and partaking of a sumptuous, filling breakfast of scrambled eggs (freshly gathered), fragrant homemade biscuits with apple butter, fresh cream, and canned cherries, they set out on their way again, having promised each other to repay the Batsons in some special way once they figured out what that might be. Mary Jane was so talented with her hands and in the kitchen that it was hard to come up with something she could use and enjoy. Maybe, they speculated, they could get a doll for Judy (who, throughout their entire visit, had not spoken one single word, at least not in their hearing).

On their departure Mary Jane had thrust into their hands two jars of canned cherries, a loaf of homemade bread, and, wonder of wonders, a small tub of butter. "Just keep it out of the sun," she told them. They thanked her profusely and headed down the road again.

They speculated about how My Ted had succeeded with farming where so many others were failing. Another of Susan's gifts was her acute powers of observation, and she had seen irrigation ditches at the edges of the fields. The rows of corn were spaced close together, perfectly aligned. Tall grass waved in another field—hay for the livestock in winter. A bank of trees protected the house from the scalding sun and the winter wind. Batson, it appeared, was using very up-to-date farming methods, allowing him to survive if not to thrive. And Mary Jane used all her skills to make the most of the resources available to her on the farm.

But Lois had the soul of a skeptic. After a long silence, she remarked, "We were really lucky, though. They could have been anybody. They could have robbed us, or worse."

To which remark Susan laughed heartily. "Farmers are good people," she said when she had recovered her speech. "They just want to do their work and live their lives. And it's a tradition with farm folks to be hospitable and share their food. My parents always did."

"Still…we spent the night in the home of complete strangers. We were taking a chance."

"How can I convince you? They were just being good hosts. They would have been offended if we had turned them down. What's more likely is someone coming to their door who wants to harm them. They took a chance with us."

Lois seemed to be giving that comment further thought. Eventually she said, "When you live in the city you learn to be wary of strangers. One thing my mother did teach me was never to talk to someone I didn't know. Even in Leadville, small as it is, she didn't trust people she didn't know."

"Then you missed out on a lot of interesting conversations with nice people," Susan replied. "My parents often invited strangers to have meals with us. We met some amazing folks. I could tell you stories about some of them. After Mama died, Papa carried on the tradition. He would give hoboes who passed by a day's work and feed them; once he helped a whole family. He gave them gas and food and a chicken, for the eggs. That's how we got Enrico, you know. He came for a handout and stayed for a job."

"Wish I'd known your parents. Mine were very particular about the company they kept."

"And yet you talk to strangers every day at the store."

"That's different. They're customers. "

Her cryptic comment brought an end to that conversation. Lois concentrated on her driving for many hours afterward. Susan supposed she was mulling over what they had discussed. It was a source of great comfort to her that, like her parents and brother, Lois never resorted to anger or sarcasm when the two of them had different opinions about a topic. She presented her thoughts and ideas; Susan did the same, and they seldom resolved their disagreement, but neither was burdened further by it. They just let it go. Given her upbringing, Lois surprised Susan with her equanimity.

Lois had come upon a bit of a challenge managing Theda's speed. A lever on the steering wheel adjusted the speed, but it was hard to set it while driving. Finally, on their second day on the road, she mastered the technique, and Theda settled into a steady pace. That meant for a somewhat more comfortable ride, even though the jouncing jarred their bodies mercilessly. Susan thought Lois seemed less tense than she had been on the first day. She knew Lois loved to drive Theda, but all day was a long, long time, and they were often coming upon something unexpected.

Dust was a huge problem, they soon found. Although small and light, the truck raised clouds of dust as she trundled down the road, at times enveloping them enough that Lois had to stop for a while, brush down the radiator, and let the dust settle. Lack of rain had made the dirt roads hard-packed and relatively smooth, but that didn't keep the dust from rising to bedevil them. Despite the heat, they both soon draped their necks and faces in scarves to keep the worst of it away. Lois was driving with only her eyes showing, which made conversation difficult.

Day Two was anti-climactic, another hot day in the unrelenting sun, more small towns, some peopled, some apparently not, deserted farm houses and barns deteriorating in the harsh prairie weather. They picnicked on a bench in front of a store with a sign, General Merchandise, which was weathering gently away, swaying back and forth in a gentle, warm breeze. No one was about. Peeking in, they saw no merchandise on the counters; dust and spider webs were everywhere.

To their great relief, they found accommodations in the back of the store, unlocked and curiously clean, though there were no towels. But the water was running, and the toilet flushed. This encounter was an eternal mystery, never to be solved. Who owned the building? Where were they? Why was there running water? They found a hand pump outside of another store which produced clear, apparently potable water neither brackish nor rusty. Lois, who had a touch of the mystic in her soul, took that as a harbinger of good fortune ahead.

Ah, but where were they going to spend the night? This time they would surely need to camp. But as darkness began to gather, they saw lightning flash across the sky and decided once again to seek shelter, this time a long-deserted barn which was home, they quickly discovered, to a nest of lively mice, a colony of fat feral cats (no doubt keeping the mouse population in check), a family of raccoons, and one very large owl. Neither of them was the least bit squeamish, although it might be surprising that Lois, the city girl, was unfazed by the animal life around them. Clearly, Lois was not the sort to be frightened off by creatures so much smaller than she was.

"Are you okay with this?" Susan asked as they inspected their temporary lodgings. The roof seemed to be sound; no rain dripped through, so they would be dry that night.

"One of my brothers delighted in teasing me with every small creature he could find. He would dangle snakes in front of my face, put mice down my back, and catch squirrels that he would pinch so they would squeal. I determined very young not to let it show that he scared me. I figured if I didn't react he would stop doing it."

"Did that work?"

"Not until he was a teenager." Lois sighed and stretched her arms and back. "Let's check out this hotel and see if we can find a good place to bed down."

They carried their bedrolls up to the loft, then went back down to secure Theda. Even though no one seemed to be around, and the house that had once been close to the barn was long gone (the foundation stones and chimney remained, but that was all), they followed their agreed-upon tasks to discourage intruders. Standing on the bumper, Susan carefully removed the distributor wire while Lois covered the bed with the tarp. Together, they threaded the rope through the grommets and Susan made her magic knot. At the last minute, she had decided to use a padlock as well (the key was on a chain around her neck), so she locked the knot, satisfied that they had done what they could to deter thieves.

Settled down among the wildlife, they were soon soothed to sleep by the owl's soft, rhythmic hoots. If rain came in the night, they did not hear it. In the morning they dug a fire pit with their handy light shovel (congratulating themselves for having thought to bring it), surrounded it by rocks, and then considered what to do about firewood. Since the barn was quite rundown, they were able to loosen enough small boards from the stalls to build a fire without, they assured each other, doing any structural damage. After all, they did not want to harm the animals' cozy home. The fire was sufficient to make their coffee—one cup each, black—using water they had pumped earlier in the day. They breakfasted on more canned peaches, slices of cheese, and the last of Mary Jane's bread and pronounced the meal a feast. They painstakingly covered the fire pit with fresh dirt until every last spark was extinguished, then dug another pit behind the barn, which they carefully covered up again once it had been used. (Another new experience for Lois, one which made her grimace but which she performed with good grace.)

Stopping after half an hour or so to refill the gas tank, they went into the small general store—open, rather to their surprise—and bought a loaf of bread. Lois had decided it was prudent to stop at every gas station they came upon. The owner of this little station also had maps of Kansas for sale, so they bought one of those as well. Pleased with the sales, he brought them each a cup of water fresh from his well and shared the key to the facilities (which were, Susan noted, quite clean and neat, with a fresh towel). The owner, however, was reluctant to let them move on; a garrulous man, he must have been lonely, seldom having customers from afar, and he wanted to chat. Finally, Lois thanked him and said they needed to get going.

Late that morning they arrived at the border with Kansas. A small rectangular sign welcomed them to the Sunflower State. Sure enough, sunflowers lined the road—which was in no better condition than it had been in Colorado, still rutted, narrow, and unmarred by informational signs, but the border crossing felt like progress. Three more days, Lois predicted, to connect with Route 66. They were both beginning to feel the heat. At home, summer heat was dry. It could be scorching midday, but it always cooled off after the sun went down. The farther east they went, the more humid the air became. They found their clothes clinging to their skins. Sweat dripped down their faces and between their breasts. Underarms were a lost cause. The seats got sticky with their perspiration. For both of them, this was a new and not necessarily enjoyable experience. Even after the sun went down the air did not cool off much, and in the dead of night it did not drop the thirty to forty degrees they were accustomed to.

Little bugs as well as sizable ones seemed to be everywhere.

"How do people stand this all summer long?" Susan moaned.

"I suppose you get used to it, but boy howdy, I don't think I could."

Susan speculated about how the pioneers must have felt, bouncing along in their covered wagons—no breeze to stir the air, no relief from the heat day or night. The women wore long dresses with petticoats and such underneath; the men had long pants and long-sleeved shirts. How in the world had they coped? It must have made them a little cranky, she surmised, and a little short-tempered. And the poor children! They were probably miserable, being heavily clothed as well. There was no ice for cooling drinks, the sun was unrelenting, and they had no place to bathe off the sweat. Tough people, she decided, tough and determined.

"Well, if they could do it, so can we," she said out loud.

"What in the world are you talking about?"

"The pioneers. I was thinking about how uncomfortable they must have been in heat like this."

"Ah," said Lois.

That day, venturing farther into Kansas, they saw more small towns and then a most unusual sight that brought Theda to a dead halt. A whirling dervish that appeared to consist of dust moved rapidly across the open land. Then another, on the other side of the car.

Still a third, on the road ahead of them.

"I've read about those," said Susan. "They're called dust devils, and they are like miniature tornadoes, only they just blow themselves out."

"Well, they sure are scary," Lois said, watching the formations dissipate. Indeed, the area was quite dusty; they saw no cultivated land nearby, only abandoned, weed-filled fields. Susan nodded her head. Then, just as Lois was about to start driving again, another amazement materialized on the horizon: a herd of about a dozen wild ponies thundered across the road, tails flying, ears back, legs churning, as if they were being chased. "Last thing I thought we'd see around here, "Lois remarked. "I know," Susan agreed. "Where in the world did they come from, and where are they going?" That mystery, like the working restroom, was never solved, for the horses quickly vanished into the horizon, and they never saw them again. Lois didn't even have time to get out her Kodak. (She had, of course, taken pictures of the barn and some of its inhabitants, although the owl proved to be camera shy. She did capture one dust devil, though.)

"Whew!" said Susan, wiping her brow. "It is boiling hot." She shrugged off her shirt and rolled her trouser legs up to her knees. Lois did the same, chuckling. "What a sight we are," she said. "Good thing there's nobody around."

Truer words were never spoken (oops…another cliché, but it fits the situation). The land around them seemed to be utterly deserted. Susan tried not to be intimidated by the vastness of it. "The pioneers didn't have maps to guide them or roads to travel on. They just followed the sun and the stars and never knew what was ahead. I've never been this far from civilization before," she mused. "It's a little frightening. I'd really like to see some signs of life—human life, that is. On the farm, we always knew the neighbors were just a couple of miles away. And we had the animals to keep us company. According to the map, we're coming to a town in about five miles, I think. Let's hope there are some people there."

Suppressing the urge to go on in that vein, Susan took a few sips of warm water from her canteen, chastised herself for having such silly fears, and settled back into her seat. Lois concentrated on driving. Theda ticked along peaceably enough. And in a few miles they did indeed come into a small town. Susan thought the main streets in these little towns looked a lot alike, with their rows of little shops, many of them with benches in front, their stillness, their compactness. There was always a main street, the road through the town, and a few side streets heading in either direction. There was usually a general store and gas station, always a post office, often a few businesses like a car repair shop or a farm supply store. They rarely saw sidewalks. There was invariably a church with a steeple, too. In one town they saw signs in front of a tiny log cabin advertising a museum. What the focus was they could not discern, for the sign said only "Museum."

In this town there were people, a few—two bearded old men, spitting tobacco, sat in front of yet another General Merchandise store; three boys sporting smudged faces and wearing ragged, dirty clothes tossed a torn baseball around, and one of the largest women (wide and short, which emphasized the wide) either of them had ever seen rumbled down the sidewalk, swaying from side to side. They looked at each other to avoid staring at the walker.

"Let's try for the general store," said Lois, parking Theda next to the curb. She got out, stretched her long frame for a moment or two, and walked up to the door of the store.

"Don't open until 10," said a voice in her ear. She jumped at the sound and turned around. The very large woman stood there, implacable and unreadable. Friendly? Hostile? She couldn't tell. Susan would never desert her friend, so she came to stand beside Lois. Just in case.

"Oh," said Lois. Susan consulted her father's pocket watch, carefully pinned to her shirt front. "An hour and ten more minutes," she said. "Unless the time is wrong. It might be earlier in Colorado."

"You from Colorado?" said the woman. "Why in the world would you come out to this godforsaken place? You crazy?"

"We're on a road trip," said Lois. "We're on our way to Chicago."

"Whatcha want to go there for?"

"To see the sights," said Susan. She held out her hand. "My name is Susan Mayfield. Pleased to meet you."

Appearing somewhat taken aback, the woman held out her large, calloused hand and gripped Susan's firmly. "I'm Ida," she said. "Ida Hornby. 'Tis almost 10 here in Hill Town." (The travelers looked around but could not see so much as a small bump in any direction). Ida nudged the two tobacco-spitting men. "Here, you two, get up and let these gals sit down. Go play pool or something." Somewhat to the two women's surprise, the men obligingly rose from the bench and ambled off. Both were wearing faded coveralls and plaid, short-sleeved shirts, along with ragged straw hats. Lois's fingers itched to take their picture as they waddled away, but that would not be polite. She held out her hand. "Lois Parker. We're from Denver."

"You don't say. You're a long way from home."

"To answer your question, we aren't crazy. We're just young and adventurous."

Ida turned and went back down the steps. "Back in a minute," she said. In a little more than a minute she returned bearing a large pitcher and two glasses. "Have some lemonade, "she said, holding out the glasses. Lois and Susan thought they had never tasted lemonade so good. "Wherever did you get lemons to make this? It's fabulous," Lois declared.

"My son in Californy sends 'em to me ever year."

Lois let out a long, satisfied sigh. "Best lemonade I ever had." Her comment drew a smile on Ida's broad, plain face that made her look almost pretty.

Just then a very tall (taller than Lois, and that's pretty tall), thin man tromped up the steps and inserted a large key in the door of the store. When it opened Lois and Susan stepped inside, Ida right behind them. The store was a wonder to behold, for the shelves held an extraordinary variety of goods, higgledy piggledy, in no order whatsoever. Hanging on the back wall was a breathtakingly beautiful quilt even prettier than the one on Mary Jane's guest bed, with an intricate design that was clearly meant to tell a story. Susan gasped at the wonder of it. "Who made such a marvelous quilt?" she asked the proprietor. Ida ducked her head. "That's one of mine."

"She wins blue ribbons at the county fair every summer," the tall thin man said. "She's the best quilter around these parts, bar none." Ida poked his arm. "Luther, stop boasting." She turned to the two women. "Luther here's my other son," she said. Susan had to carefully compose her face to hide what came to mind. That woman, who must have weighed close to three hundred pounds and was not much taller than Susan, was the mother of the cadaverous man beside her? How could that be? Wonders never cease, she told herself. So instead of expressing that uncharitable thought, she turned to Lois and said, "We simply must have a picture of that quilt. Is there enough light in here?" "I don't know," Lois replied, "but I can try." The sun slanted in through the dirt-streaked windows, making the possibility of a good picture more likely. She snapped two pictures, choosing the angle that gave the most light, and hoped they would come out. Even in black and white, the quilt would be stunning, but Lois would color it when she got home.

The travelers bought a few supplies, but before they got on the road again Ida plied them with a homemade cherry pie, a jar of lemonade, a jar of dill pickles and a jar of homemade raspberry jam. "Bless you," said Ida. "You've cheered me up no end, going on a trip like this. If the good lord can send us someone like you two, maybe there's hope after all. You are a sight for sore eyes." (The same words, Susan recalled, that Mary Jane had used.) Ida was, to their relief, not a hugger like Mary Jane (one could get smothered by Ida's bosom, Susan thought), but she kissed each one of them on the cheek and sent them on their way full of good cheer.

These people, Susan noted, did not seem disconcerted by the extreme heat. They moved around with a reasonable degree of energy and their clothes were not wet with perspiration. But then, she reflected, they had all that cool lemonade to drink and shade to sit in.

Later, during their picnic lunch in a small, shady park a few towns eastward, Lois resurrected the discussion about strangers. "I'm not saying all strangers are potentially evil," she said after a bite of her peanut butter sandwich. "But there are bad people in the world. You never know who they are, or where they are."

"Of course there are bad people. And right now, with the Depression, there are desperate people too. People who would do almost anything to get food or protect their families. But I get feelings about people, and my skin crawls when I come across bad ones. I just seem to know."

"How about good people who are desperate, though?"

"I prefer to start out believing that people are basically good, and if you appeal to their decency, they won't harm you."

"That's pretty naïve of you, Sue."

"It's gotten me this far, though, and I don't plan to change any time soon."

Lois smiled and nodded. "That's part of what I love about you. You're so generous about people, and so kind. I have a ways to go before I am as good as you are."

Silenced by Lois's compliment, once back on the road Susan gazed at the landscape they rolled past and thought her private thoughts.

When night fell they were near another small town (the faded sign read "Peculiar, Kansas," a colorful name to say the least). They chuckled about it, concluding that it was no more peculiar than any other small town they'd seen thus far, then decided to look for a likely camping spot that would be close to people but not in the midst of the town. They soon found one, another one of those small parks, this one on the edge of what Susan labeled KSR#19 (the 19th road they had been on, K for Kansas, SR for State Road—Susan had created and refined a small-town cataloguing system; she was a born organizer). The park's grass had dried up, but there were two trees in full leaf, a picnic table with benches and a fire pit, and a pump for water. What more could they ask? The ground was flat, there was plenty of room, and the wind was still. Before leaving they had practiced setting up the tent, and they both felt confident they could manage it. Probably, however, they should have had at least one more practice run. Still, what could possibly go wrong?

Plenty, as it happened. First, their disparate heights made it challenging at best to stretch the tent to the right dimensions. That accomplished after much difficulty and a few well-chosen words on Lois's part, they could not find all the stakes. While Lois held the tent upright as best she could, Susan searched through the back of the truck in vain, finally coming upon the missing stakes in a pile on the far side of what passed for a hill in that area. Why in the world had they been set down there? She let herself feel a moment's annoyance—not at herself or Lois, just general, all-purpose irritation— and then got on with the task at hand. Once the stakes were in place, they had to be hammered into the ground. Easier said than done. Lois was strong but not as strong as she imagined herself to be. No matter how hard she struck the stakes, they refused to budge. When she paused for a break, Susan picked up the sledge and began pounding. Reluctantly, the stakes succumbed, and the tent was at last secured. Never one to toot her own horn, Susan smiled and said to Lois, "I'm sure they were just about ready to go in." Lois shrugged. Pride had never come between them, and they were not competitive with each other. "I'm sure you're right," she said with a slight smile. "Good for you, though." She put an arm around Susan's shoulder. "Let's get on with it."

Growing up on the farm, Susan had developed powerful muscles that belied her small frame. No one would suppose her to be that strong, but she had helped pull calves, built a chicken coop, guided a plow through the soil, and accomplished many other tasks in her days as a farmer's daughter. On a farm, everyone had to pitch in, and they became the stronger for it.

Get on with it they did. That experience had educated them about what to do and what not to do; it would surely be easier next time. The tent secured, they ate a cold supper, used a small pit dug for a specific purpose, there being no outhouse, and retired for the night. Susan curled up into her bedroll and fell asleep almost instantly, but Lois felt assaulted by the prairie's night sounds—insects chirping ceaselessly, creatures rustling through the dry grass (despite what she had told Susan about being nonchalant when her brother tortured her with a snake, she dreaded snakes and hoped that was not what she heard), birds settling into the branches of the trees, and from farther away, an eerie, haunting howl. Fear curled around her heart. Living in a big city, she had long since come to terms with being afraid and determined not to be without good reason. Of course she took precautions, being sure to stay away from the worst parts of the city, not going out alone at night (her artist friend always picked her up and brought her home), and teaching herself some defensive tactics in case of attack. In these bad times, people down on their luck sometimes took unwise chances. Knowing that, Lois was careful, but she had schooled herself not to be fearful or spooked.

Until she was lying on the hard ground inside a tent which provided no protection whatsoever against sharp-toothed predators on a dark, starless night, and some unknown creature was caterwauling into the blackness. She finally fell into a restless sleep and was relieved and happy when the sun woke her at dawn. Susan sat up in her bedroll and smiled. "Coyotes howled last night," she commented. "They woke me up, but I went back to sleep."

"Coyotes? What kind of creatures are they?" Surprised that her friend didn't know about coyotes, Susan described them. "They're rather like dogs, about the size of a boxer but really lean and fast. They sometimes hunt alone and sometimes in packs. Sounded like a pack last night."

In the great, isolated vastness of the prairie when Susan confessed to being afraid, Lois had comforted and reassured her. Now it was Lois who needed comfort and reassurance. "Scared me to death, Sue," she said. Susan didn't downplay her friend's fear. "They could attack people, I suppose, but they usually don't. We're too big for them. They look for small prey like hares and rodents. If they were in a pack, they were after something a little larger, maybe a deer or an antelope. Not us. But they usually don't run in packs. I don't know why those were, last night. They must have been after some large prey."

Lois squared her shoulders. "Every day on this trip I am learning something new," she said. "It's as good as a graduate degree."

One of the best aspects of Lois, a part Susan especially loved, was her ability to rebound from an upset and just get back to everyday life. She didn't let past mishaps or mistakes drag her down. She faced life head on, an admirable quality in Susan's view. Lois was quick to forgive and forget and never held grudges. Susan aspired to be more like her.

Camping is much harder than I thought it would be. Only sheer stubbornness got that tent up. L was a little afraid of the coyotes at first, but I remember hearing them on the farm. We could hear them most nights. Papa was worried that they would get into the hen house, so he used barbed wire around it. I wonder what's become of the farm; he was always so proud of it, he worked so hard, and I hate to think that it is just disintegrating into dust, but that's probably what's happening. I don't think I can bear to go back there. Good thing it's not on our route.

Chapter Seven—On to Missouri

When they stepped out of the tent that morning something indefinable had changed. The air was disturbingly still, even stiller than before, the humidity thick and oppressive. The clouds hung low, dark and menacing. No sounds came from any direction. Wordlessly, they set about their morning routine. Breakfast was Ida's blue-ribbon cherry pie. No coffee; they chose not to build a fire. They did the necessary and refilled the pit with fresh soil, then struck the tent, which proved considerably easier than setting it up had been. Lois, the tall one, tightened down the canvas tarp and off they went, heading east toward what should have been the sun but was instead a dreary, gray, somehow menacing dawn.

(After a couple of nights on the road, Susan had taught Lois to remove the distributor wire since it was so hard for her to reach into the engine. Susan then took on the task of loading the back of the truck and tying the tarp down; Lois tightened the rope. They had achieved a rhythm in their routine.)

After they'd been driving for an hour or so, expecting to see the sun any minute (for there had been nothing but cloudless blue sky thus far on the trip), their surroundings grew much darker. The stillness was smothering. They determined they had no choice but to keep going, so Lois kept Theda on what she hoped was the road. In moments that seemed like hours, they emerged from the eerie atmosphere into a sight unlike any either of them had ever seen before.

Debris was all around them: broken pieces of wood, a tin roof, intact but upside down, the remains of an old outhouse on its side, a cracked window still in its frame. They saw loose bricks, parts of a fireplace, and a twisted bed frame standing on end. Scattered here and there were large tree branches and smaller twigs, though they had not seen any trees for miles and miles. Lois got out of the truck and started taking pictures. "You've got to see this to believe it," she declared. "I do believe we just went through a tornado."

"I wonder why we didn't get blown clear into the Land of Oz," Susan said, a slight smile on her lips. "Look at the tarp, Lois. It's still tied down just the way you fixed it, and we're still on the ground. Theda is untouched." Lois grimaced. "It's weird," she said. "Really weird." She shook her head and climbed back into the driver's seat. Why they were spared became another unsolved mystery to add to the list Susan (an inveterate list maker) was keeping in her journal.

In the aftermath of the storm the air was washed clean, the humidity less cloying, the heat less oppressive. A slight breeze stirred around them when they stopped to step out a short while later. It was refreshing, calming, a return to a something resembling normal. Susan took in a deep breath and stretched her arms above her head. Lois followed suit.

In due time they came to a cluster of dwellings. A sign greeted them: Hallelujah! Kansas. Pop. 121.5. A short drive took them into Hallelujah! which they discovered was inhabited, thank goodness. There was the ubiquitous General Merchandise store with a bench in front and a single gas pump, a café, a post office, an American flag flying gaily in the slight breeze in front of it, and, wonder of wonders, a paved main street along which they saw a few one-story houses, an auto repair shop, a drug store and three churches of varying denominations: Catholic, Baptist and Methodist, to be specific. Even more wondrously, all of the stores appeared to be open and doing business, as they saw a few cars and trucks parked on the street, one of them next to a horse-drawn wagon. The town had not been touched by the tornado; everything was intact.

They decided to fill up the gas tank and buy some supplies at the general store. Lois pulled up at the single pump and the door of the store opened. Susan looked up, and up, and up, to see a very tall, very slender man peering down at her. His brown eyes were warm and intent; they matched his lovely, burnished-brown skin, which covered his lanky frame very elegantly. He had pitch-black, wavy hair and high cheekbones. His face was clean-shaven, unblemished. She thought he was the most beautiful man she had ever seen.

"Can I help you?" he said, addressing Susan. "We need to fill up the gas tank," Susan replied, thinking that this man would be perfect for Lois; he was tall enough, but Susan would really rather not have it work out that way. Never jealous, never competitive, the two friends would come to an agreement, but it would be painfully hard for Susan, for she felt an instant attraction to this man and was certain he felt the same about her. The unseen connection, the spark, had crackled between them and she knew deep down that he was as aware of it as she was. Her heart zinged.

Lois, however, was paying no attention to the clerk whatsoever. While he filled the tank, she went into the store and started gathering supplies, noting the sign that read "Crandall's General Store." The store was a throwback to another age—a potbelly stove in the middle of the room with a cushioned rocking chair on either side of it, flowered curtains on the windows, barrels of what must have been flour and other dry commodities here and there around the room. The shelves were filled with jars and cans of various types and sizes, produce (what little there was) was displayed unseparated on one long shelf, and a small refrigerator probably contained milk and eggs. Of a meat counter there was no sign.

Behind the cash register stood a woman of average height and bronzed skin like the man outside. Her black hair was mostly concealed underneath a colorful head scarf, with just a few strands peeking out here and there; despite wearing no makeup, her features were clearly defined—especially her deep-set, intelligent brown eyes which surveyed them with friendly curiosity. When she smiled she showed beautiful, even white teeth. "Can I help you?" she said, echoing the attendant outside. "Are you finding everything you need?" She spoke in a low, musical voice with a noticeable accent. Lois responded with a smile and a nod. "I think I've got what we need for now," she said, bringing her purchases to the counter. "I'll pay for the gasoline as well."

At that moment the tall man and Susan came into the store. They should have looked incongruous side by side, even ridiculous, but to Lois's surprise they actually looked just right together. "Ravi," said the woman at the counter, "how much for the petrol?" The last time they had bought gasoline, it was five cents a gallon. The tank had taken all 10 gallons. "Half a dollar," said the man they now knew as Ravi. Susan stepped up to the counter. "I'm Susan Mayfield, and this is my friend, Lois Parker. We're going to Chicago on Route 66."

The woman put out her hand. "Pariz Crandall," she said. "Welcome to Hallelujah!" Susan was burning with curiosity about the "Pop. 121.5" sign and what in the world an immigrant (from India, she surmised) was doing smack in the middle of Kansas, USA, but she was too well bred to ask. She only shook Pariz's hand and said, "We are very pleased to meet you."

The man stepped up to the counter. "Mum, how about serving these young ladies some tea?" Now they knew a little more—the gorgeous man was Pariz Crandall's son. So—Ravi Crandall. There had to be an American father involved in this family. Susan wondered where he was, but again, she did not ask.

Mrs. Crandall nodded and escorted them to a private parlor at the back of the store, separated from the front by a beaded curtain in the doorway. Hot though it was outside, the room was cool, with an overhead fan running gently and heavy, colorful draperies blocking the western sun. All four walls were lined with bookshelves, full of all kinds of books, many of them with titles in an unfamiliar script. Susan felt her heart skip a beat. Mrs. Crandall served them green tea along with a confection not familiar to them but very tasty—sugary, slightly spicy, and quite rich. The three women sipped their tea in silence for a few moments; Ravi went back out to tend the store. Then Pariz Crandall spoke. "You are curious," she said. "You wonder what a woman like me is doing in a place like this, but you are too polite to ask."

Susan and Lois waited for her to continue, which she did after a

63

few more sips of tea. "My husband, Ralph Crandall, came to India with his Lutheran missionary parents as a child. My mother was the family housekeeper. Ralph and I grew up in the same household. I was to marry the man chosen for me by my parents and his, but Ralph and I decided we wanted to marry each other, so we eloped and came to America." She paused, wiping tears from her eyes. "My parents disowned me," she said. "I had dishonored them. But Ralph honored me by joining my faith. We have been happy together."

She took a sweet from the plate in front of her and ate it delicately. "As for coming here, Ralph's father died in India of a fever and his mother and sisters returned to Kansas, where they came from. Mother Cordelia had some money from the missionary society so she bought this store. She ran it until she died two years ago." She grimaced. "Out in the middle of nowhere." She wiped her mouth with a napkin and said, "I don't know why I'm telling you this, two total strangers. It's just that I don't often have friendly women to talk to. Women do come into the store, but they keep their distance. I'm different, and they don't seem to want to get to know me. Perhaps they are put off by my accent. You seem like nice young women and I felt comfortable with you right away; I wanted you to know more about us." Pariz Crandall's English was precise, correct and educated. She spoke it with a British flavor, and her "t's" became "d's".

Lois did not hesitate to ask: "What about the sisters? Where are they? Couldn't they run the store?"

"Oh, no," Mrs. Crandall replied. "They are both in Africa. They are Christian missionaries. Ravi is our only child. He will take over the store when the time comes." Lois and Susan exchanged a quick, ironic glance. Couldn't Ravi's mother see the hypocrisy in that?

"Where is your husband today, Mrs. Crandall?"

"He went for supplies. It takes two days to get to Wichita and back again. He should be home tomorrow."

"Pardon me for saying so, but I wouldn't think you'd have much business in a small town like this one."

"In truth, even located where we are we do quite well. We are the only store in a twenty-mile radius that is still open in these hard times. We've been able to keep going because we didn't have all our money in a bank."

Susan, growing bolder, inquired about facilities and was directed past the parlor into the rest of the small dwelling, where she found a pristine bathroom. She sat on the toilet after flushing it. Her heart was pounding. Love at first sight—that was just a fairy tale, wasn't it? But it had been there, that magical something, between her and Ravi. He was Mr. Right; she was sure of it. Still, she dared not say so in front of his mother. She was not sure how this would work out, but something in her was confident that it would. No matter how many times she told herself she was being foolish, the feeling would not go away. If she knew it and felt it, she was certain he did, too.

After they had drunk the tea and eaten a few more of the sugary sweets, the travelers knew it was time to be on their way. One more day in Kansas, they hoped, and they would be at the border with Missouri. When they stood and announced their intention to depart, Mrs. Crandall went to her compact little kitchen and came back with a packet of what looked like bread except that it was flat. "Take this naan bread along with you," she said, "for good luck on your journey. Blessings to you on your way."

On the road again, they discussed their Hallelujah! Kansas encounter. What an unusual place, and what remarkable people! Despite their unspoken, mutual understanding of unstinting honesty, however, Susan failed to mention her instant attraction to Ravi and his to her. She held it close to her heart, choosing to wait for the relationship to unfold in its own good time.

"What do you think now about talking to strangers?" Susan asked after a while.

"I'm still learning every day," Lois replied. "Small town people seem to be as friendly as farmers."

"They don't see strangers very often, so when some come through town, it's a real treat. There was a small town about 10 miles from our farm where we went to get supplies, and the people who lived there always wanted to sit down and have a 'chin wag,' as Mama called it. They brought out food and drinks and loved to have long chats. I guess small-town people are pretty much the same no matter where you go."

Let it not be said that these two daring young women were insensitive to the conditions prevailing in their state and in their nation. As they were setting up camp that night (much more efficiently) in a sheltered grove not far from the road, Lois remarked on how fortunate the Crandalls were to have been able to keep their store open in such a place, so far from any center of commerce or industry.

"So many abandoned farms we've seen," Susan murmured. "I guess I didn't really understand how bad things were until we started out on this trip. It's so sad, Lois."

Lois nodded her assent. "It is truly tragic. People going hungry everywhere, children without enough to eat — it makes me feel sick at heart. But it also reminds me just how lucky we are."

"Do you think Mr. Hoover will get reelected? People are blaming this on him."

"Franklin Roosevelt is running for president. It's definitely time for a change. I voted for Hoover last time, but I wouldn't do that again."

"Your family is rich. You probably haven't had much experience with really poor people like the ones we've met so far. People barely hanging on, but they share what they have. They make the most of their resources, whatever they are. I think they are amazing."

"Just because my father made a lot of money before the crash doesn't mean he's still that rich," Lois said. "He salvaged most of his investments by moving them overseas, but he and Gloria have had to tighten their belts, too. He made money on silver, true, but he lost a lot in the crash. And treatments for her…"

Susan said nothing more. She knew that trying to dry out Lois's mother must be expensive (and, as far as she knew, totally ineffective). Still, the Parkers were far better off than the Mayfields. Scrabbling for a living on the farm had been hard enough before the crash, and Clyde had not had a good crop for a couple of years before that; she had assumed he stayed at the farm because he didn't know where else to go or what else to do, but it certainly was not a money-making proposition in the best of times.

Later in the day it began to rain. Neither of them had ever seen such a downpour, sheets of water blinding the driver and obliterating the road, lightning flashing right above them or so it seemed, thunder that sounded like cannons blasting away. For a short while Lois endeavored to work the windshield wiper, which was on the driver's side and had to be operated by hand, but she quickly gave up and pulled off to the side of the road. When the rain finally stopped, what seemed like hours later, they started to get out and discovered that they were surrounded by slimy, moving mud. Moreover, Theda was sinking fast. "We are mired in mud," Lois said, stating the obvious as she sometimes was wont to do. Susan climbed back into the cab, which of course was completely soaked from the rain, and got out her journal notebook, silently congratulating herself on having secreted it carefully in her handbag so it stayed dry. Writing took her mind off the dire situation they had found themselves in at the moment.

They were both completely drenched, everything in the cab was wet, and the truck was well and truly stuck. She decided to write something hopeful, to cheer herself up, while Lois stood on the running board and surveyed the situation.

Maybe Lois is beginning to trust people and risk a little more. When I consider how she grew up, the parents she had, it is amazing that she is so cheerful and outgoing. It makes me realize how lucky I was with my family. Hard work, yes, but so much love and goodness. (However, Lois is not very cheerful at the moment, I must admit. What a dilemma!)

Chapter Eight—Mired in Mud

Lois looked down at the mud. "Well," she said. "Hmm." She got back into the cab.

For the first time since embarking on their wild adventure, they were stumped. "I guess we just have to wait for the mud to dry," said Susan.

Lois said, "Hmm" again.

After what felt like hours but was probably no more than half an hour or so, the sun came out and the clouds disappeared. However, they were not much cheered, because it was clearly going to take a very long time for the mud to dry enough that they could even walk somewhere for help. Neither of them was given to tears or hysterics, thank goodness, but this was a dilemma worthy of a dramatic flair if ever there was one. There was nothing to say, so they sat in silence and waited. Lois told Susan she looked like a wet poodle, and Susan replied indignantly that Lois looked like a beached seal. That led them both into gales of healing laughter.

They had just begun to recover their breaths when, like a mirage, a vehicle came into view on the horizon, a conveyance drawn by two sturdy-looking horses. As it got closer they saw that the horses were pulling what appeared to be a small trailer with a chain on it. A very large man stood at the front of the trailer guiding the reins. Soon the enormous beasts were right in front of Theda.

The man got down and tapped on the windshield. Lois opened the door. "Stuck, eh?" he said (he too was stating the obvious). Lois nodded. "Oh, yes, we sure are." They both chose to ignore the slight smirk on the big man's face, although they could imagine what he was thinking. Helpless women...

"Chloe and Bertha'll have you out of there in no time," he declared, and he slogged through the muddy mess, his heavy boots sinking several inches. With what looked like no effort at all he hefted the chain, hooked it up to Theda's undercarriage, and snapped the reins. "Haw!" he shouted. The powerful horses began to pull. Even with all their supplies to weigh her down, Theda was light; it only took a few minutes for the huge, immensely strong animals to release her from the sucking mud. Lois watched their muscles straining and was overcome with admiration. She had never known that horses were so strong. The ones at the dude ranch were tough, but they wouldn't have been able to do that.

Back on the road, which was still very muddy but nothing like what they had been stuck in, the truck slid around a bit but soon steadied. Their rescuer had not undone the chain. "We'll get ya to higher ground," the man said.

And they did. At the top of the next hill the road was much drier, passable even, and they could see that it was drying out ahead of them. Lois got out of the truck. Tall as she was, the man was taller. He had a broad chest and large face decorated by a long white beard.

"Thank you," she said, watching him unhitch the chain. "You saved us. We didn't know how we were going to get out of that fix!" These sturdy horses were much different from the ones she had known at the ranch—they were wide, with hefty, tufted legs, large hoofs and broad heads. They seemed docile enough, but my, they were strong.

"Seen ya from my barn," the man replied. "Hitched up my team and came right fast."

Susan spoke from the cab. "I never saw such big horses," she commented. "What kind are they?"

"Clydesdales," he replied. "Best horses in the world. Beat these smokin', gas-guzzln' critters ever time." He inclined his head toward Theda. Susan and Lois introduced themselves and asked the farmer if they could do anything to repay him for pulling them out.

"Name's Caleb Schmidt," he said. He pointed to the south. "House is up there. You're welcome to come and set a spell if you like. The missus would be mighty happy to see some females. Not that many of 'em around here."

How could they turn down such a generous invitation? They followed the horses to the farmhouse, which sat high up on a hill. Lois parked Theda and they went into the house, reveling in the smell of fresh-baked bread. Both took off their shoes, as did the man of the house, before venturing inside. To their left they saw a woman who completely filled the kitchen doorway from side to side. Not as tall as her husband, but considerably broader. She smiled, a wide grin that lit up her plain, square face. "Caleb. Where in the world did you find these two gals?" She gestured toward the parlor on their left. As Caleb Schmidt relayed the story of the rescue, Lois and Susan sat in the horsehair chairs on either side of the fireplace and exchanged a glance. Once again they had landed in a nice home with good people. Susan let out a long, slow sigh. Lois lifted her eyebrows in reply.

It was indeed fresh bread, just out of the oven. Mrs. Schmidt, who introduced herself as Martha, served the bread with hot coffee, creamy butter and cherry preserves. Heavenly. "Just a little while ago," said Lois, "we thought we were stuck in the mud until the road dried out, which could have been days! Your husband came along just like a knight in shining armor."

Martha let forth a laugh that shook her whole frame. "Ain't you a stitch?" She held out the tray with the bread and coffee. "Have another slice. You gals are way too thin."

Lois, thinking the kindly couple were owed an explanation, embarked on a brief recitation about who they were, where they came from and where they were going. Martha could only shake her head in wonderment. Her husband, who had taken a chair farther away from the fireplace, was snoring tunefully. "He sure ain't no knight," she said, "but he's a good man."

"He must be a good farmer too," Susan remarked. "Making it in these hard times." "The Lord's taken good care of us," Martha said. "We've fared well. Caleb's a dab hand at farming, and I take my baked goods to town to sell once a week or so. People like good fresh bread and pies. Yes, we've been blessed." The three women chatted about inconsequential things for a while. Susan noticed cross-stitchings with religious sayings on the walls, and above the mantel was a painting of Jesus, with a cross hanging above it. Clearly, these were deeply devout people.

When Caleb Schmidt woke from his nap and announced he was going out to rub down the horses, they knew it was time to leave. Though she didn't say so out loud, Lois was a little down-hearted at the prospect of camping out when it had rained so heavily, but they needed to move on. She asked Martha about accommodations.

"Fifty mile or so from here there's a motor hotel. Dirt cheap, fifty cents a night. Might be wise to bed down there," Caleb said when he came back into the house. He had seen the camping equipment on the truck and seemed to have read her mind. "Well worth your money," he added. Lois nodded in agreement. She had been thinking the very same thing.

Once they got back on the road, again plied with culinary bounty — a full loaf of Martha's fresh-baked bread (for which she refused payment), a jar of plum preserves and a mightily tempting-looking rhubarb pie — they found the surface dry enough to travel on without problems. Lois, who did not often talk when driving, commented, "He sure felt smug and superior, didn't he?"

"I don't care," Susan said. "He came along and saved us. We've been so lucky. How long can our luck hold out?" To which statement Lois chose not to reply. They rode in silence for a while, until coming upon KSH#21, name unknown, where they saw the motor hotel Caleb Schmidt had spoken of. It was named, imaginatively, U Drop Inn, and they noticed only one car parked in front of a unit. There were six small units, each with a separate door, ranged along the roadside, with a larger building at the west end. Lois parked the flivver, retrieved a dollar bill from her concealed cache, and went in to book a unit. She returned a few minutes later, key in hand, and moved Theda in front of Unit 2.

The sight they met when entering was a new one to Susan, although Lois had a few times in her wilder days stayed in such a place: a double bed sat under the curtained window that looked out at the road. A wobbly wooden table was flanked by two equally wobbly-looking chairs, and next to the table was a quaint woodstove which had two burners, storage doors above the burners, and an oven below with a door that opened sideways. Beside the stove was a pile of firewood; opposite was a small sink, next to it a counter covered with linoleum. The floor, which creaked, was also covered with cheap, brown, patterned linoleum. The room was tidy, though, and the bed was neatly made. Susan envisioned another night clinging to the edge of the mattress; still, that would be safer and more comfortable than the bedroll inside the tent. Lois retrieved a box of various foodstuffs from the back of the truck; Susan set to work to cook dinner. She'd had long experience wrestling with a woodstove and soon had a good fire going. Along with Martha's bread, they would have warmed-up canned meat, canned pinto beans and rhubarb pie. A veritable feast, every scrap devoured gratefully by both of them. The pie was stupendous, memorable. A county fair winner for sure.

"They seem to be very religious," Susan remarked as she was clearing the dishes. "We could send them a picture of the Mount of the Holy Cross."

"Good idea," replied Lois absently. She was busy studying the map spread out on the table in front of them, trying to figure out exactly where they were. Lois had inquired about the name of the town and was told it was called Barker's Crossing, but they couldn't find it on their map, leaving them with a rather vague idea of how close they were to Missouri. Both being practical souls, they concurred that they would know more in the morning, finished cleaning up from dinner, and headed for bed.

Morning dawned bright and clear, not a cloud in the sky, a view that greatly cheered them both. Susan brewed coffee and they enjoyed more of the magnificent pie before packing up and starting on the road again. They had not gone far, though, when Susan told Lois to pull off to the side of the road. "Why? What's wrong?"

Susan, who had exceptionally sharp hearing along with her keen eyesight, had heard a noise she had long been familiar with. Living on a farm, she had often heard injured dogs moan in distress; she and Clyde found abandoned dogs near the farmhouse every few months. They always took them in, restored them to health, then tried to find good homes for them. Shep, a beautiful collie once he'd been cleaned up and restored to health, had stolen their hearts, so he had stayed, but the others had gone to new families. There was for Susan no mistaking that sound. She got out of the cab and started to walk along the ditch beside the shoulder of the road. Soon she found the source of the pitiful noise—a small, very dirty dog lay curled in a miserable ball in the ditch. He was soggy, far too thin, and shivering with fear. She knew better than to reach toward him or try to pick him up when facing him. She had to do it from behind. Back at the truck, she found a towel and walked around behind the dog, quickly scooping him up into her arms wrapped in the towel. He looked up at her and seemed to understand that she was friend rather than foe, for he relaxed a bit as she held him. She returned with him to the cab.

"What on earth..." Lois said when Susan and the dog climbed back in. "Whew—that dog smells awful."

"He was in the ditch. I don't think he's hurt, just wet and scared. He needs a bath. We have to stop as soon as we can and get him cleaned up." "As soon as we can," Lois agreed, wrinkling her nose. She was not unsympathetic toward the small wiggly creature, but Lois was meticulous in her person and in her dress, and she disliked dirt in any guise. After the dog was cleaned up, though, Susan was sure Lois would view the little fellow more kindly.

Lois watched intently for a good place to pull off the road. They would have to use some of their radiator water to wash the dog, but it was a necessary sacrifice. Soon enough they came to a spot with a clear space off the shoulder. Susan hopped down with the dog and set to work as soon as Lois brought the water. In the midday heat the water was warm; the dog made no protest as Susan scrubbed the mangy fur, discovering that the little guy was white with black spots here and there. He was about 16 inches high, Lois guessed, a dog of many origins. His short coat was curly and thick; his ears perked straight up on his small head, and his face resembled that of a poodle, Susan thought. Not a bit like Shep or any of the dogs she and Clyde had rescued at the farm. The eyes, partially hidden by hair, were brown, very keen. He seemed to be taking in everything around him. His long, feathery tail began to wag.

"Someone dumped him, I'm afraid," said Lois. "What a rotten thing to do to a helpless animal."

"I want to keep him," Susan replied, picking up the dog and hugging him to her. "He is awfully thin. We need to give him something to eat."

"What do dogs eat?" Lois had never had a pet of any kind. This was all new to her.

"Meat, mostly. We fed Shep table scraps and sometimes gave him a bone with some meat on it. Let's break out a tin of corned beef and see if he likes it. And he needs water, too."

He did like the food, devouring every scrap placed in front of him on one of their small tin plates in no time at all, then lapping up the water. "Well," said Lois. "I guess we've got ourselves a dog. What shall we name him?"

"He looks rather like a teddy bear to me. Let's call him Teddy."

"Teddy it is. Now we'd best be on our way."

With Teddy cozily perched between them, they set off down the road again. They had not gone far, though, when they saw a car by the side of the road. A man was standing beside it, waving frantically. Lois pulled up beside him and stopped. It flashed through her mind that this might be a trick, aimed at robbing them of their vehicle—or something worse—so she didn't get out of the truck. Susan opened her door. "What's wrong, sir?"

The man, who was lean and gaunt, making him appear even taller than he was, wore ragged coveralls and a tattered shirt. He was waving a red kerchief. His face was deathly white.

"My wife," he said. "She's in the car. She's having the baby. We were on our way to the next town to get help, but she said to stop. Thank god you came along." His language was that of an educated man, his face clean shaven and his hands clean and smooth, not like those of a farmer. "I have no idea what to do."

Susan, the country girl, had assisted at many births, but never that of a human being. However, she got out of the truck, walked over to the car, and peered in. Sure enough, a woman lay curled across the seat, moaning. Her face was contorted with pain, her belly distended. She clearly needed help.

"Get some towels," Susan told Lois. "Bring some water in a pan." To the husband she said, "Do you have anything for the baby? Cloths? Blankets?" He nodded and walked around to the back of the car. Their belongings were tied to the top. He untied the bundle and began digging among the contents. Susan climbed into the car. It was a tight squeeze at best; small though she was, she had to crouch beside the woman. "I'm Susan," she told the woman. "Tell me your name."

Around a gasp of pain the woman replied, "Annabelle." Then she grasped Susan's hand and squeezed so hard it hurt. When she relaxed Susan released her hand and reached for the towels Lois was holding out to her. She tucked some towels under Annabelle and checked the birth canal. "Can't be that much different from a cow," she muttered under her breath. The baby was indeed coming; amid the blood she could see a small, shiny head covered with black hair. Reaching in, she found a shoulder and turned the body slightly to make the passage easier. "Just like a cow," she repeated. In what was probably only moments but felt like hours, the baby slid out from its mother, quickly followed by the afterbirth.

Susan was somewhat alarmed by the amount of blood, fearing the mother could bleed to death, but the bright red flow stopped after what seemed like forever but was no doubt only a few minutes. She breathed a sigh of relief. Some blood was normal, she knew; cows bled when they gave birth.

There remained the umbilical cord, which must be cut in such a way as not to cause infection. Susan paused to ponder. Then she called to Lois, "Hand me your little service knife and get the first aid kit out of the truck, please." With commendable foresight they had kitted out first aid supplies with a small bottle of mercurochrome, which would do to sterilize the knife. She cut the cord and tied off the stump; the baby didn't make a sound. Susan's anxieties about dealing with a difficult birth had been soothed. Except—the baby needed to start breathing, which hadn't happened yet.

The tiny chest was still. Susan's heart pounded with fear. Was the little girl (for it was a girl) dead? Gently, she rubbed the baby's back and after a few seconds was gratified to hear a coughing breath. The baby was as tiny as a doll, but alive. Thank god. Now there remained only the cleaning up to do—of the infant and of the mother.

She wrapped the child in a soft blue baby blanket and handed her to her mother, who looked up, her eyes filled with tears. "What's your name again?" she asked.

"Susan. Susan Mayfield."

"Susan Mayfield, meet Susan Dawson. She and I will never forget you."

Susan was nonplussed. To have a child named after her—what an honor! What a delight! She climbed back out of the car into Lois's waiting hug and breathed a long, deep sigh of relief. "I wasn't sure I could do it," she said after a moment. "Then I told myself, 'It's just like delivering a calf' and I was okay."

"You were a trooper," Lois said. "A real trooper." Released from the cab, Teddy raced joyously around Lois's legs. Susan leaned down and picked him up, nuzzling into his warm, clean body.

The man had gotten into the car and was admiring the most beautiful baby ever born—at least, that's what he told his wife. Lois and Susan were getting ready to leave when he got out again and came over to them. "You saved Annabelle's life," he said. "I'm such a dolt when it comes to things like that. I can't thank you enough. We'd heard there was a midwife in the next town, and that's where we were going." He paused for a moment then held out his right hand.

"I'm Reginald Dawson," he said. "Annabelle and I are on our way to St. Louis where I am hoping to get a job at the Missouri Botanical Garden. I am a trained horticulturist and was working at a nursery in Pueblo, Colorado, but the funding was withdrawn so we had to leave to seek other employment. We had planned to get to St. Louis before the baby was born, but it seems she decided to come a little early. We can never repay our debt to you. Thank you from the bottom of my heart." He reached into the back of the car and brought out a small plant, a beautiful miniature pink rose in full bloom, and handed it to Lois (since Susan's arms were full of Teddy).

"Perhaps this will help you remember us," he said.

"Oh," said Susan, "we could never forget you." She set Teddy down and reached into the cab to get her journal and tore out a page. "This is our address in Denver. Please write to us and let us know how you get along."

Dawson nodded in agreement as he climbed into the driver's seat. "Water it once a week, not too heavily," he advised. "It likes full sun and a nice warm place to sit. With good care, it can last you many years. Don't plant it outside, though. It needs to be inside in the cold weather."

"I hope they will be all right," Lois said as the couple drove away. "That baby was early, wasn't she?" Susan nodded. "About four weeks, I'd guess. But the mother was starting to nurse her when I got out of the car, and I'm sure the wee one will get loving care. I just hope her husband finds a job. What nice people they are."

Once again, the two travelers had come upon good people, decent folks just trying to get by, and for the first time they were able to offer help instead of needing it. That felt deeply wonderful.

What a time we've had! Stuck in the mud and being rescued by horses, finding Teddy (oh, how I love him already), helping bring a new life into the world! And most of all, I have met the man I want to marry. He is gorgeous, with that beautiful smooth skin, those marvelous brown eyes with the longest lashes I ever saw, those dimples, that smile. And he is a kind, good man, a gentleman. His house is full of books. Awfully tall, but I can forgive him for that. I can just picture myself melting away in his arms. I imagine him to be a wonderful kisser, a gentle lover—oh, I am getting ahead of myself. I have no idea whether he feels the same way, or what his mother and father would say if he did...But I know I am falling in love. And I think he was attracted to me too. In fact, I'm sure of it.

Chapter Nine—Pure Bliss

Teddy stuck to them like glue. Even though they didn't have a collar or a leash for him, he showed no inclination to look for greener pastures. Moreover, he was a gentleman, waiting until the opportunity came along to do his business, not drooling on the car seat, and eating almost daintily. He sat upright when Theda was on the move, peering straight ahead, ears perked up and tail wagging ever so slightly. Susan was glad he was not a large dog, for that would have left her with very little room. Teddy was just the right size. In spite of the heat, she liked the feel of his warm body snuggled up against hers.

Dusk was gathering when they saw a rather battered sign that excited them both: Campground, it said, and an arrow pointed to the right. Eagerly they followed the arrow and found a wondrous sight, a fully equipped campground with designated spaces for tents that had smooth ground, a picnic table and fire pit, parking space for cars, and–oh, bliss!—a low concrete building that contained restrooms and men's and women's showers along with a deep galvanized steel washtub for laundry and a water pump outside. They were in transports of delight; both had gotten rather grubby; their clothes badly needed washing, and the prospect of a refreshing shower was almost too much to bear. Lois, for one, feared that she smelled a bit rank— but then, so did Susan, so neither had commented on the other's odor.

A sign on an iron table requested $1 to camp for the night, with what looked like a metal toolbox to put the money in through a slot in the top. The box was padlocked, but it would have been easy to pick it up and cart it off, Lois thought. Then she saw that is was bolted down to the table and would have been challenging to remove. She slipped in the dollar.

Except for the two of them the campground was deserted. Four other camping spaces awaited occupants. Neither of them commented on being alone in the campground, but Susan was a little uneasy.

To date they had not set up the tent so quickly. They had learned each other's strong and weak points and how to take advantage of strengths. Lois had gotten adept at pounding in the stakes, while Susan set up camp, unrolling the bedrolls, building a fire and opening tins of food (not forgetting for a moment, of course, to feed Teddy, who waited politely for his meal and a good long drink). They heated up contents of some tins over the fire pit and relished the meal, which while not fresh food was nonetheless hot and tasty, cleaned up the camp and damped the fire, and, leaving Teddy in charge, headed for the shower.

While Lois showered Susan guarded her clothes, making sure the money stash was safely secured in the brassiere pockets specially fashioned for the purpose. For her part Lois could have stood under the water, even lukewarm as it was, for hours, but that would not be fair, so she ceded the throne to Susan, guarding her clothes in turn while she enjoyed the treat. Then they washed clothes and the towels they had used during Annabelle's labor, hanging them about on tree branches until they were dry enough to fold and pack. In the cloying heat, that did not take too long despite the humidity. Collapsing onto the bedrolls, they wished each other good night and promptly fell deeply to sleep.

Toward dawn several sharp barks followed by a low, fierce growl woke them. Was that Teddy, who had chosen to stay just outside the tent flap? What on earth? They rose simultaneously, Lois picking up the baseball bat, and peered out. What they saw was at once amusing and unsettling. Teddy had his teeth firmly clamped on the pant leg of a medium-height, skeletally thin man who was working to break open the lock on the tarp rope to get at what was inside. A grimy newsboy cap sat low over his brow. His clothes were almost in tatters. "Get that critter off me!" he screeched.

"Why should we?" said Lois. "You are trying to rob us."

"I jest want sumpin to eat," he replied sullenly, kicking his leg out at Teddy. The dog hung on.

Even in the dim light they could see that the man was skin and bone. What harm could he do them? Susan walked over to Teddy and spoke to him softly, and the little dog released his hold on the tattered pant leg. "You could have just asked," she said. The man said nothing. "Ain't et fer four days," he said. Just then he sank down onto the grass. Susan went to the cab and brought out a box of crackers (they always kept a supply of edibles in the cab; he could have just looked in there), a jar of peanut butter (another reliable staple) and a knife. She handed them to the man. "Take these and be on your way," she said. She gestured toward the facilities building and added, "There's a pump there where you can get drinking water." He reached for the food with one claw-like hand and smiled, showing a mouth almost devoid of teeth. "Much obliged," he said. After a few minutes of eating crackers and peanut butter he managed to get up and walk away. Susan hugged Teddy tightly to her chest. "What a grand dog you are!" she told him. In response, he licked her nose.

They watched until the man disappeared from sight. "I feel guilty, as if we should have done something more for him," said Susan.

"What else could we have done?"

Susan shrugged. "I'm not sure. But peanut butter and crackers won't feed him for very long." Lois nodded. "That's true, but I still don't know what else we could do to help him." "I don't either," Susan replied. "I just wish…" And she let the subject drop. For she knew Lois was right—there really was nothing they could do to help. So many people like that one, hungry, homeless…The travelers were caught up in a tragedy not of their making and not within their means to alleviate. Awake anyhow, the two young women made breakfast, broke camp in the starlit, silky dark, and started out once more, sobered and silent. The man had indeed been desperate, just as they had discussed earlier, but clearly he was in no condition to do them any harm. Susan, with her muscled arms, Lois, with her tall, solid body, could have had him on the ground in no time. His was one face of desperation, one among thousands upon thousands.

For the remainder of the day each harbored her own thoughts about the hungry man and the multitudes like him. Susan could not get the image of him out of her mind—his craggy face, drawn thin to his bones, his stick-pin arms and legs, the desperate look in his sunken eyes. Lois balanced her anger at his attempt at thievery against her pity for the homeless drifter. She wondered what had brought him to such a terrible circumstance. Where had he come from? Where was he headed? Did he have loved ones? Even though she knew there would never be answers to her curious questions, they crowded her thoughts, forcing her to constantly redirect her concentration to the vehicle and the road ahead.

She spared a thought for the little dog, too. She had not been overly eager to invite him to join their traveling troupe, but that morning he had proved his worth 200 percent and then some. She resolved to treat him more kindly. Not that she had been unkind, really; just that she had not made much effort to befriend him. From now on, she resolved, she would.

After the eventful morning, the rest of the day held no further surprises or alarms. They encountered no one on the road in either direction, the sky remained clear and blue, and the scenery was pleasant, the countryside featuring gently rolling hills, green grass and here and there a few animals grazing. Theda obligingly rumbled down the road without protest. After a time they found a shady, grassy spot to picnic and enjoyed the last of Ida's bounty. Susan studied the map and calculated they would reach Joplin the next day if they had no more mishaps. "Maybe we can find lodging tonight," she said.

"Good idea," Lois answered, "but we might have to sneak Teddy in. Some places don't allow dogs." Thanks to the generosity of people they had met along the way, their cash supply was better than expected, so they could afford a night in a cottage court. Already Teddy had become a permanent fixture in their lives, and neither of them had brought up the question of what would happen when they got home again, for their landlord had a strict no-pets policy. Privately, Lois told herself, "One worry at a time. We'll face that when the trip is over."

That night they stayed at a small, nondescript motor lodge which cost $1 for a stuffy, boxy, crowded room with only a wimpy little window fan to fend off the heat. Off to the right was a decent-enough bathroom—clean at least, though the towels were as thin as paper—but the room contained only a bed, a dresser and one chair, no stove or icebox. They chose a room at the far end of the building and slipped Teddy in under a towel. Even though they hadn't seen a sign restricting pets, they were taking no chances. Gentleman that he was, Teddy was perfectly behaved, quiet and calm. Lois told him what a good boy he was, getting a vigorous tail wag in response. They made a cold meal from a tin of baked beans (which Teddy ate with gusto) and the remains of Ida's bread, showered, and fell into bed, grateful not to be out under the stars when thunder began rumbling late in the evening and they heard rain pounding on the tin roof. At least the roof of the tumble-down building didn't leak. With commendable foresight, Lois had parked Theda under an overhang and hung her bedroll over the canvas top on the exposed side of the cab; they hoped that would keep the cab from being too wet in the morning. Susan was so exhausted she didn't even write in her journal. She promised herself she would record the remarkable events of that day, just not right then.

In the morning they found the cab somewhat wet but tolerable when they put dry towels on the seats. After a breakfast of canned meat (shared, of course, with Teddy) and crackers, they started down the road again. Another day, more miles under their belts. All that day the sun shone relentlessly and the heat was intense, heat waves shimmering off the road—which, to their amazement, had suddenly become paved. They passed through Wichita, Kansas, stopping only for gas and replenishment of staples that were running a little low. Wichita was a mid-size town with an Old-West feel, not unlike Denver. Lois gracefully maneuvered the flivver through the streets, avoiding hazards of all kinds including pedestrians oblivious to traffic, and brought them out to the other side. Wichita was not as noisy as Denver, they agreed, but it was also not as pockmarked by closed businesses and empty buildings as other places they had seen. Treating themselves, they stopped at a café on the outskirts of town for a cup of coffee and a meal of egg sandwiches and green salad, plus a plump sausage for Teddy, and then started on their way again.

They arrived in Joplin late that night, around 10 p.m. according to the pocket watch. Weary, thirsty and sleepy, they took in the sights with blurry eyes. The main street was lined with motor hotels, and they soon found one to their liking. It was a little more expensive at $1.50 a night, but it did have a private bath and a small kitchenette— just a stove, a sink and a table with two chairs and an oilcloth table cover in a garish flowered pattern. They had to supply their own cookware and utensils, but they were used to that. And they did indeed have to bring Teddy in clandestinely, wrapped in a couple of big towels this time; a sign prohibiting pets was clearly visible at the front desk. Good fellow, Teddy made not a peep and settled contentedly between them when they went to bed.

Morning brought a more cheerful aspect to both of them. Susan recorded the events at the campground in her journal; to her, that felt like shedding a burden of sorrow and guilt. Lois, more open with emotions than Susan, had said her piece aloud and was ready to move on. They enjoyed a good breakfast and were soon on their way to seek out Route 66.

Joplin, a historic town, had a population of about 30,000 people according to a booklet Susan had bought beforehand and was showing the effects of the Depression. They saw closed businesses, run-down houses and the ubiquitous bread line, but they also saw expensive cars, large, luxurious-looking homes and the beautiful Carnegie Library. People slumped here and there on the library steps, some holding out tin cups in hopes of a handout. Pigeons wandered around the building and commandeered the sidewalk in places. At the edge of town they saw a small "Hooverville," a makeshift village where people used discards of all kinds to create shelters—cardboard, car parts, pieces of metal, discarded furniture, scraps of lumber. Several shacks had only one piece of furniture visible, either a rescued seat from an abandoned car or a broken-down sofa. Children played in the dirt. Mothers hauled water from a nearby stream. Men kneeled, many of them smoking cigarettes or pipes, silent and grim. Not a happy scene. When they came upon Route 66, toward which they'd been driving for days, they both sighed with relief to be on the road again. The motor hotel had been comfortable enough, and they had succeeded in slipping Teddy in and out, but they were eager to get headed toward Chicago.

Route 66 was a revelation. For one, the highway itself was much wider than the ones they had been traveling on. It was mostly paved even though the pavement was rutted and uneven in places; small town after small town appeared along the road, and they began to see Burma Shave signs, which entertained and amused them. Lois, of course, had to stop and take a picture of an especially catchy one now and then. Luckily, the flivver was slow enough to be able to read each sign as they ambled down the road.

POLITICAL PULL/ MAY BE OF USE/FOR RAZOR PULL/ THERE'S NO EXCUSE/BURMA SHAVE

Freight trucks, which could go considerably faster than Theda, often hurried past them, heading north, honking their loud horns. Once or twice they saw a truck hauling cattle to market. The city girl was upset by the sight; the farmer's daughter took it in stride.

The road, Susan had read, was 16 feet wide. Though paved, it had no shoulders on either side.

In places train tracks ran alongside the road. Open freight cars often held more than freight; they could sometimes see the men who had come to be called hoboes—aimless travelers who hopped the freights that carried them from town to town. Their appearance was distinctive, different from that of the men in bread lines and on the street: These men wore baggy trousers with several pockets that bulged with uncertain contents. Most had large, floppy hats and flapping open jackets, even in the heat. Their mark of distinction, though, was a stick with a bundle tied at the end, flung over a shoulder as they walked along. Some also had colorful bandanas around their necks. At one place where Lois stopped to fuel up, they saw a "hobo jungle "not far from the tracks. A group of men huddled around a small portable stove; a pot of something simmered on top. There were no tents or temporary structures of any kind, but it was clear that people had been camping there, for the ground was strewn with discarded tin cans, liquor bottles, cigarette butts and other debris, and in places the soil was indented where bodies had lain to rest. Both of them shuddered to see how these rough men were living—yet the men sounded jolly enough with their chatter and laughter.

Lois and Susan had known there was a hobo jungle on the outskirts of Denver, but neither had seen it, for it was to the south, along the river, where they did not typically venture. Hoboes tended not to come into town, so the sight of this camp along the railroad line was new to them. Before they left on the trip Susan had done some reading up about the life of a hobo and learned that it was highly precarious. Being a hobo was dangerous. Hopping a moving train carried the danger of a misstep, which could throw the hopper under the train's wheels as it passed by. Railroad officials, called "bulls" by the hoboes, hounded these itinerants. When found, they were thrown off the trains, not gently.

There were other hazards. Some men had been crushed to death when a load was dumped into the car—ice was particularly deadly—and they always risked being run off by sheriffs or policemen when they camped. It was a hard, hard life—nonetheless, there was solid community among them; they gathered together whenever possible and shared food and what shelter they could accrue. Often, two or more walked the tracks together. Susan was moved by their plight—though not enough to approach and offer them food. Lois, while not unmoved, was apprehensive. Some hoboes were known to be violent, she had heard. Best to keep their distance.

Fortunately, the road was dotted with gas stations which did not look too rundown. Gasoline was cheap, as low as four cents a gallon. They enjoyed chatting with the attendants who filled the tank. (Theda was not greedy with fuel, which they appreciated, but she had to be refilled frequently.) Lois often paused long enough to take a picture of a station; they were unique, each one colorful and different. Some of them boasted garages which offered automobile repair and labeled themselves service stations.

When nightfall arrived, they decided once again to sleep indoors. A motel (new word they had taken to—they'd seen it several times along the way) named U Stop Inn caught their eyes. Surprisingly, pets were allowed so they didn't have to sneak Teddy in, which was good. Like other places they had stayed, this unit had a kitchenette, allowing for a hot meal followed by a good night's sleep. Lois took a picture of the building, which was shaped somewhat like a large upside-down bowl and colored a very visible bright red.

Entering the Missouri countryside, they came upon a landscape quite different from what they had seen thus far. There were green meadows, fully leaved trees waving in the breeze, even wildflowers along the roadside. Cows munched on grass, birds of prey flew overhead, and the air smelled sweet. They saw people working in fields, tending to crops which seemed to be thriving. The heat and humidity did not abate, but somehow they were more manageable amid such scenery. Joplin was on a river confluence, which provided nourishment for the soil and ample water for crops and livestock. No drought was apparent there.

Susan calculated it would take three days to get across Missouri and two more to get to Chicago. "We're going to be gone longer than two weeks," she told Lois when they had settled into a campground after their first day in Missouri. "We'll use more than a week just to get to Chicago, and then we have to get home again. Maybe we can find a faster route on the way back." Susan began fretting about her job; Lois seemed nonchalant and unconcerned, although the prospect of running low on funds did trouble her, a concern she chose not to burden Susan with since her friend was already anxious. If need be, she resolved, they would work for a few days along the way to get enough money to make it home. They could wait on tables, clean houses, cook—she was not unduly worried. Vigorous young women would be able to get some kind of temporary work;

Road Trip

she was sure of it. As for their jobs, Lois was pretty certain their bosses would wait for their return before looking to replace them.

Life, they agreed, always seemed brighter in the morning. They brewed coffee, fed and watered Teddy, and ate rather dry pastries purchased the day before at a truck stop. They could see farmhouses in the distance between towns.

Hoboes—what a sight. We fed a pitiable hungry man yesterday but when we saw the hoboes we got as far away as possible. Lois is right; they could be dangerous. Altruistic impulses don't always end well, and I'm afraid I can be a rather impulsive person, a trait I might need to work on refining a little. It could get me into trouble. Thank goodness for dear Teddy, though; whatever did we do without him? He has completely attached himself to us and taken on the role of guardian, for which I am eternally grateful. I don't know what we shall do when we get home; I doubt the landlord will let us keep him. Well, if he won't, we'll find some place that will, that's all. Teddy has secured a firm and lasting place in my heart.

I must expand on the astounding events of a couple of days ago, when on a single day we got stuck in the mud and pulled out by two enormous horses, found Teddy in a ditch and rescued him (how fortuitous that was!), and brought a new life into the world. I do wonder how the Dawsons are faring, and if they have made it to St. Louis. Has he found a job? How is my tiny namesake? She was so very small. Will we ever hear from them again? What a strange adventure that was. I've helped deliver calves and lambs, even a litter of pigs at a neighbor's farm once, but a human infant—that was my first and, I hope, my last. Should I have the good fortune to bear children, I sincerely hope someone who knows more about such matters than I do will be there to help me. Then there was the poor downtrodden fellow who tried to break into the money box at the campground. I fear he is not long for this world.

Chapter Ten—Never What They Expected

With so many hours on the road, Susan feared she would get bored and Lois would get tired. But in fact the reverse occurred—there was so much to marvel at, so much new to see, that the miles seemed to fly by. They found a picnic spot along the road after passing through Springfield and were munching away (Teddy too) when they heard a low growl, low in the throat. Teddy had tensed, every muscle alert, ears pricked high, and was looking intently at a man lurching toward them. He waved a bottle in one hand and held the other to his chest, a la Napoleon, inside his tattered shirt.

"Stop right there," Lois said, standing and facing the intruder. "You're drunk. Go away." Backing up her bravado, Teddy strained at the rope that tied him to the picnic bench. But the man kept walking toward them. He was about average size, thin, unshaven and unsteady on his feet. Then, without making a sound, he fell straight forward onto his face. The bottle flew from his hand and rolled away. Susan took a tentative step toward him.

"Oh, lord, Lois, he's not breathing. What should we do?"

Lois looked around. No one was in sight. "Well, we can't just leave him here. I think he's dead, Sue." Her face had gone unnaturally pale. She knelt down and felt for a pulse. Finding none, she said, "We need to go to the next town and find a sheriff or somebody."

"Why did he die?" Susan's voice quavered. She had never in all her years actually seen a dead person. Dead animals, sure. But a person? When her mother died at home, her father had kept her away from the house until the sheriff came and took away Mama's body. Death in the house, but she had not seen it firsthand. She felt ill.

"I have no idea," Lois replied, bending down to feel for a pulse, "but he is definitely dead." Cleaning up from their picnic, they left the man where he had fallen and headed to the nearest town. Susan, the farmer's daughter, who had seen considerable death among the animals, was shattered by the sight of a dead person, while Lois's courage in a crisis rode to the fore. She stayed calm and resolute. They went to town and found the sheriff.

He was disinclined to believe them. Two agitated young ladies telling a fantastic tale about a dead man? Ridiculous. They were probably imagining the whole thing. But they were insistent, so he reluctantly followed them back to the spot where the man still lay, still very, very dead. Upon seeing the body, he knelt and examined it. He turned toward them, holding open the man's shirt. "This here's what killed him," he said, pointing at a bullet wound near the heart. "Someone shot him. Got a gun?" He stood, put one hand on his holster and walked toward the truck. He appeared prepared to search for a nonexistent weapon, perhaps having decided they were the culprits. How easy that would have been for him... "You seen him comin' at you so's you shot him," the sheriff muttered as he walked.

Lois took a stance in front of the truck door, one hand on the handle to hold it closed. He could not know how her legs were trembling inside her utilitarian trousers, or see her hand shaking as she grasped the door handle. But her voice was steady. "Sheriff, I told you, he came at us waving that bottle around. We never saw him before in our lives, we do not have a gun or any other such weapon, and we are on a road trip to Chicago. You are welcome to search if you like, but you won't find anything." As for searching the truck, Teddy had other ideas. When the lawman got menacingly close to Lois he growled again. The shcriff, who had not even had the courtesy to tell them his name although his badge said O'Reilly, spun around at the sound. "Keep that dog away from me," he snarled.

The women were truly in a fix. They had reported the death, the correct thing to do, and now they were as good as being accused of causing it by a narrow-minded man who obviously did not like women in any guise—or dogs, for that matter. Susan picked Teddy up and cuddled him close to her. "He won't bother you," she said. "But don't you need a warrant to search our truck?"

He paused mid-step. "This here is the scene of a crime. I need to search everything around here."

Susan stood her ground. "Our truck is not part of the crime scene," she said in her firm librarian voice, the one she dredged up when patrons got noisy. "If you don't leave us alone, we are going to start screaming for help." Other picnickers had pulled in by that time and were seated at tables a little farther away, studiously trying to ignore the melee going on near the Model T. "Someone will come. They always do." The sheriff looked around the area, appeared to ponder several possible scenarios, and shrugged his shoulders. He gave Susan a hard look, then reluctantly turned away from the truck. "Get the hell out of here," he said, "and don't come back." He turned toward the dead man, knelt down beside him, and started looking in his pockets.

Resigned to never knowing who shot the man or why (another mystery forever unsolved), relieved to have gotten away from a sticky situation, Lois and Susan got into the truck with all deliberate speed. Lois drove away sedately; neither of them looked back. For a time, the memory of that frightening experience kept them silent, each considering what she might have done differently, each coming to the conclusion that she had done the best she could under the circumstances. At length, their natural sunny natures came to the fore again. They were on the road, on their way to Chicago; they were young and carefree, and they had dealt bravely with another frightening situation. All had, for the moment, ended well. Susan kept patting Teddy, who sat complacently by her side. "Aren't you glad we found him?" she said after a time. Lois merely nodded; she was concentrating on driving. Traffic, mostly trucks, had increased, and she needed to keep her entire attention on the road ahead.

The road was still a narrow ribbon with no shoulder on either side, paved with asphalt in places and ground-down dirt in other places. Weeds festooned the edges of both sides of the highway. Here and there a dandelion brightened the scenery. The straight stretch seemed to go on into infinity.

BIG MISTAKE/DRIVERS MAKE/HIT THE HORN/NOT THE BRAKE/BURMA SHAVE

"However," Lois commented after a time, "now you must concede that not all people are nice, and that treating them as if they were decent doesn't always work."

Susan had, reluctantly, to cede the point. The sheriff had been a most unsavory sort, ready to pin a murder on them if he could have gotten away with it. He was neither respectful nor pleasant. In fact, Susan decided, he was downright nasty.

I thought we were in real trouble for a minute there. We didn't let that man bully us, though. But if there hadn't been other people around, he might have arrested us even though we had no gun— thank goodness there were. I still believe in the goodness of most people, but I have to admit there are a few rotten apples in every barrel. We met up with one today. We have been so, so lucky on this trip; something scary was bound to happen, I guess. Let's hope that's the last of it.

Chapter Eleven—
Maneuvering Through Missouri

Their first encounter with Missouri had not been a happy one, almost being arrested for murder. They could only hope things would look up. The countryside was somewhat greener than they had seen in Kansas, but mosquitoes and some kind of almost invisible insects seemed to be everywhere, buzzing and hovering and biting. They decided they could not camp out under such conditions. Not feasible at all, what with the dampness that never lessened, the evenings and nights that didn't cool off, and the constant presence of bugs, what the locals called "no see 'ums." They would just have to economize on food.

Fortunately, motels seemed to pop up all along the route. They noticed some gas stations that were deserted and rusting away, but enough were open to keep Theda on the road. Stopping to refill the tank every couple of hours (since they never knew how much gas remained in the tank) and put water in the radiator gave them a chance to get out and move around, loosening stiff muscles and sore joints, getting water and relief for Teddy, and using the facilities. These frequent stops delayed them a bit, but it was worth it to stretch their legs and let the little dog get some exercise. Evenings were long; it didn't get dark until well after eight.

Dusk was a tricky time to drive, though, as they soon learned. Up until then, they had stopped before it started getting dark. But on their first night in Missouri they were still searching at about 8:30 for a place to lay their heads until morning when Lois suddenly brought the car to a stop. Susan jerked forward, and Teddy scrambled to keep his balance on the seat. Susan had been half asleep; she was startled to say the least. "What's wrong?" she asked.

Lois's face was as pale as Susan had ever seen it. "There's something in the road. It looks like a body." Having seen a dead body earlier that day, both travelers were naturally wary. Lois walked to the front of the car. Susan climbed out from the passenger side. Teddy immediately began sniffing the ground all around him.

Indeed, there was a dark shape in the middle of the road. At that time of night it was difficult to discern exactly what is was, but the Ford was at least ten feet away from it, in no danger of accidentally running over it in the semi-dark. Lois walked over to the shape and knelt down. Then she let out a rich laugh.

"I thought it was a person, and I was about to run over him. Come and look, Sue."

Obligingly, even though detecting a powerful stench as she got closer, Susan inched toward the huddled shape and knelt beside her friend. Heaped in the middle of the dark road lay a pile of cow chips. "It must have fallen off a truck," Susan said. "One cow couldn't have done all that." They backed away. Accustomed though Susan was to cows and their leavings, that pile was a bit much, and it gave off a strong odor even though the chips were dried out. "I caught that smell about half a mile ago or so," Lois said, "but I thought it must be from a nearby farm. It distracted me for a second or two. Then I saw that pile, and I thought sure it was someone or something dead in the road."

"You didn't tell me," Susan replied.

"You looked so peaceful, sleeping. I didn't want to wake you up unless I had to. I'm surprised the smell didn't get to you, though."

Teddy turned back toward the truck, uncharacteristically leaving their sides. Apparently he too found the odor offensive, for he seemed eager to put distance between himself and the smell. Susan followed him. "Thank goodness you didn't hit it," she remarked. "We'd never get a motel room if we smelled like that." Another excuse for a good laugh.

Lois carefully skirted the manure pile on the road when they got underway again. The lights of a town twinkled ahead of them; surely

93

they would find accommodation there. The small town had no motels, but they saw a sign on the cracked, weedy sidewalk of the main street through town offering rooms for rent. "They might not take overnighters," Susan commented, but she followed her friend up the steps and stood beside her when she rang the bell. They could hear it echo through the hallway. In a moment a tallish, thin man wearing, incongruously, a top hat and business suit, vest and all, answered the door. Susan had a brief flash that they had come to a vampire's house and started to turn away. But Lois spoke up. "We're looking for a room for the night."

"Just have one room left," the man replied, in an unexpectedly mellow voice. Susan thought he sounded much nicer than he looked. "You'll have to share."

"Oh, we're used to that," Susan said. "It's what we always do." The man, who had yet to tell them his name, pointed to the steep stairway at the end of the narrow hallway. "First door on the left," he told them. Susan slipped Teddy under her arm and held him firmly as they went up the stairs. "Buck fifty," came the voice floating upward. "Breakfast at 7 sharp." A pause. Then, "Coffee's five cents extra."

Worth it, they agreed when morning awoke them. When they came downstairs, they were led by enticing odors to a dining room where several people of assorted sizes and ages—half men, half women—sat around a large, long wooden table while one of the shortest, roundest people of indeterminate gender either had ever seen set dishes on the table dishes which turned out to contain light, fluffy corn muffins, crisply cooked sausages, scrambled eggs and delicately fried hash browns. An amazing array of breakfast delights. The coffee was delicious, too, worth the extra nickel apiece. Lois and Susan both secreted sausages for Teddy, who was stashed outside in the truck. He'd spent the night, quietly, in their room, but before dawn Susan took him out to the truck, cautioned him to be patient, and returned to their room so they could go down to breakfast together.

Conversation at breakfast was in short supply. Every now and then someone would say, "Pass the butter," or grunt in a pleasurable way, but for the most part, the diverse assemblage was silent, intent upon eating every morsel put in front of them. Lois and Susan were used to talking during meals. That was the time when they shared their day's plans, or, at dinner, the day's happenings. For them, meals were about sharing and bonding as much as about food. For these assorted roomers, meals were obviously for eating, period. The rotund man (they had determined he was a male after having a close look at his face, where a few errant whiskers sprouted) who had brought in the food spoke once as he made his way along the table with a large coffee pot, asking if anyone wanted a refill. "No extra charge," he said. Now and then a diner would hold up a cup and mutter "thanks."

Replete and happy, they set out on the road again. Once on their way, they turned to each other for a moment and enjoyed a hearty laugh. "Adventure comes in all shapes and sizes, doesn't it?" Susan remarked. They spent a few moments commiserating with the very stout man who had served them; he was as round as he was tall, and they were sure he couldn't see his feet even when lying down. Both of them had harbored an unspoken worry that he might lose his balance and topple right over. Getting him up again would take more than one person. He was, they agreed, a magnificent cook, however. They just hoped he would be able to keep it up. Neither of them had ever seen anyone so roly poly who was able to get around, much less cook. They were bemused by the contrast between the man who had admitted them and the one who had fed them. Were they friends? Partners? Surely not brothers; they were so completely different. Who knew? Another mystery never to be solved.

The humidity clung to them; the tiny bugs bedeviled them, and the unrelenting heat wore the two travelers down. The next night, nearly across Missouri (to Susan's surprise), they stopped early at a small hotel in St. Clair, near St. Louis, where they would cross the mighty Mississippi River. Though neither as interesting nor as unusual as the rooming house of the night before, the compact little hostelry was clean and comfortable, and Teddy was welcome — the owners had two dogs of their own. Both dogs were considerably larger than Teddy, but he made friendly sniffing gestures toward them and they reciprocated in kind, all tails wagging vigorously. (They had learned a new aspect of their companion's personality—he got along well with other dogs and was not the least bit aggressive.)

Neither of them had ever seen a river so wide. The South Platte River that made its way through Denver was a mere creek in comparison. The Mississippi looked to be many miles across, although Susan had read that it was only a mile across at its widest point; it was said you could not see one bank from the other where the river meandered back and forth. Beginning in Minnesota, it flowed all the way to the Bay of Mexico. Lois was prepared to stop along the bridge and take some photographs.

St. Louis seemed to move slowly, like a tide coming in or going out, sinuous and languid. Yet it had long been a center of industrial activity, commerce and trade. It had a lengthy, storied history. There was so much to see that they didn't have time for, but Susan could not leave without a quick stop at the Central Library, a magnificent structure that held a vast selection of books and the design of which was breathtaking. They were both entranced by the Michelangelo-like ceiling in the periodicals room and the sunken garden behind the building. The stunningly beautiful central hall, with its arched ceiling, awed them too. Lois tried to take some pictures, but the light was not right; she was not sure if they would work. Still, she had to try.

That detour, and a brief trip through the core of the city to admire the many glorious buildings decorating it, meant that they would be going across the Eads bridge later than they had intended to. Perhaps they couldn't get good pictures then. But the city was enormous from their perspective, much, much bigger than Denver, and they were eager to leave it behind.

Both were struck by the number of Negroes they saw in St. Louis. In Denver, dark-skinned people were a rarity, seldom seen in the areas where the two women lived and worked. Certainly they existed, but they did not often leave their favored settlements. In St. Louis,

Lois and Susan saw large numbers of them, a circumstance which Susan determined to learn more about after they were home again. Always keenly observant, she noted that the Negro men moved in small groups and were mostly silent. Some of them were doing menial jobs, like sweeping the street, while others hung around on corners smoking and talking in low voices. Women, sometimes whistled at by the men, walked briskly past groups of men without glancing toward them. Though many of their dresses looked well worn, they held their heads high and appeared neat and clean. A few even wore gloves. Here and there she saw a spectacular hat atop a head of glossy black hair.

Before the trip, Susan had brought home stacks of encyclopedic library books about the states they were going to go through, the cities they would come upon, and the towns they would go through along the way. But they had learned very little about the sizable, mistreated population of Negroes in Missouri; there did not seem to be much written about them. Now the young women were eager to find out more: Where had these people come from? What did they do to make a living? How were they treated in that big Southern city, St. Louis? The travelers knew that Missouri was in mindset a Southern state, and they both were well aware of the Jim Crow laws that prevailed in the South. Missouri had been a slave state, admitted to the Union as such under the Missouri Compromise. Schools in Missouri were by law "separate but equal"—though from what little Susan had been able to find out, "equal" was not in any way applicable to the schools Negro children attended. The Negroes clustered together as if for protection, responded deferentially to whites who spoke to them, and if they worked at all did menial jobs like sweeping the streets or collecting trash. Clearly, the situation for the Negroes they saw in St. Louis, and millions of others elsewhere in the US, was bleak at best.

Missouri had recently been battered, both by the Depression and by Mother Nature. A drought had hit parts of the state that summer and the summer before, destroying thousands of acres of crops. The farther east they ventured, the more evidence of drought they saw.

The Depression had hit St. Louis manufacturing hard; as many as a third of factory workers had been laid off. Five years before their trip the vast river had overflowed its banks, destroying rich farm soil, crops, livestock, buildings and land and killing people; thanks to the Depression which happened only a few years later, recovery had been slow to put it generously. They saw devastation around them as they traveled. Droughts and floods—a vicious combination. They could only shake their heads and commiserate with the stricken farmers, homeowners and businessmen. No doubt, they agreed, the minority population had been the hardest hit.

Wordlessly, yet both understanding the agreement, the friends decided to postpone discussion about the plight of the Negroes until a time when they knew more and could talk about it from a safe emotional distance. Both were affected and upset; neither wanted to put a damper on the trip. They had already seen enough sobering sights; there did not seem to be room just then for more.

When they got to the bridge, they were silenced by the size of the river and excited by its churning water. Even Teddy perked up. He had been unusually quiet for the last few days, not drooping exactly but clearly affected by the heat and dampness. Every time they stopped, he lapped up water like a thirsty wanderer finding an oasis in the desert.

But the scent of water enlivened his interest, and he began looking around in every direction, his nose twitching and his body quivering. Susan asked Lois to stop for a few minutes so she could record her impressions for posterity. Someday, she thought, her still-imaginary grandchildren would enjoy reading about it.

What a stunning sight it is, this river! I shall never forget this moment. The river is so wide. The water laps at the bank. People are fishing from the bank, throwing homemade poles into the water, casting and retrieving over and over again. Boats that can go under the bridge pass by, mostly barges; the traffic is as busy as a main street in St. Louis. The mixture of smells is intriguing—fish, water, dirt, smoke, and more. I can't identify all the odors. (Of course Teddy can, and many more besides...) There is a light breeze, whipping the water a little, but it's not a cool breeze. There are shacks along the river, flimsy structures to say the least. How can people live like that? What choice do they have?

Chapter Twelve—Crossing the Big Muddy

For the rest of their lives, Lois and Susan were to recall in vivid color the experience of crossing the Mississippi River that summer. The gods were with them; the sun shone down onto the river, sparkling against the water. Theda seemed not to mind the different road base on the bridge and bounced along willingly enough.

Lois saw some people parked off to one side, taking pictures, and she decided to do the same. They stopped and took pictures of each other and of Teddy, who stayed glued to their legs. Perhaps overwhelmed by the water, he made no move to sniff around or check out the territory, and he jumped eagerly back into the truck when they got ready to start up again. (Every time the truck started, Lois breathed a sigh of relief. If it came down to cranking, Susan would have to do it; she just wasn't strong enough. And Susan was so short that it seemed impossible for her to attain the necessary leverage.)

They saw all kinds of boats—big ones, small ones, boats with waving passengers, tugboats and barges. Compact little boats for fishing, canoes, flat-bottomed boats. They even saw a paddle wheel, a la Mark Twain. They were assailed by the almost constant tooting of horns—boat captains greeting each other, they concluded, or perhaps warning other boats to make way.

It was an active river, with strong waves buffeting the littler boats about. Twain had written years before that the Mississippi was a treacherous river which could take lives and which required consummate skills to negotiate because it was full of unknowns. His pen name, in fact, was a river man's term for noting depth. For not only was the mighty river wide; it was also quite deep in places. Unlike the (usually) peaceful Platte, the Mississippi river bed was not visible. They stopped a few more times so Lois could drink in the sights. And then they were across, entering Illinois.

As they prepared to traverse Illinois at an angle, lengthwise, they were heartened by the closeness of their goal. They had gained a day crossing Missouri; two long days, Susan estimated, and they would be in Chicago. At long last.

They were long days indeed. Upon arriving in Springfield, the state capital, they decided to visit Abraham Lincoln's grave and pay their respects to the man whom both considered the greatest president the US ever had (with the possible exception of George Washington). From a street vendor Susan bought a small bouquet of roses for a dime; they placed the bouquet beside the headstone. Lois captured the tomb on her camera. They stood in silence for a moment, then left with Teddy in tow. There did not seem to be much else to see in Springfield, though they did drive by the majestic state capitol building. Walking around, they saw that the sidewalks were not brimming with pedestrians, and they did see closed store fronts, yet the town looked relatively unscathed. The streets had been swept clean; they saw very little litter, and the people did not all have worried frowns. Some were even smiling or laughing. Teddy trotted along happily beside them, but crossing one street, a car came way too close to him. Susan said, "We need to get him a collar and a leash. If he saw something he wanted to chase, he could just run off, maybe get hit by a car."

They soon found a general store which stocked what they required and were much relieved to have the little dog secured. Teddy accepted the restraint placidly enough, though he strained his neck around to see what they were up to. They picnicked in a well-kept city park under a large oak tree before heading north again.

Homage to the great man paid, his city briefly seen, they set about to find a place to spend the night. Motels were more expensive in town—$2 a night, they found. But then on the outskirts they came upon a cluster of cabins built along the banks of the Lower Illinois River with a modest sign beside the road naming the place as The Lincoln Resort and offering cabins for $1 a night. "They must be hurting for business," Lois commented. "Well, those cabins do look a little rundown. But the roofs look sound, and at least we'll get shelter for the night."

The cabins had apparently been built to emulate Lincoln's original log cabin, with large logs and mortar, along with wood-shingled roofs. Each one was about the size of a large shed, maybe eight by eight. The proprietor, a toothless man who gummed a pipe, silently handed over the key to the cabin labeled "Law Office," took the proffered dollar, and pointed vaguely to his left. On the way they saw some other cabins — "Birth Place," "My Old Kentucky Home," and "Library."

Shabby though they had looked from the outside, the inside of the tiny cabin was clean and neat, with a double bed handsomely decorated by a hand-sewn quilt, a small table and one chair, a counter with a portable propane cook stove on top, and a wash basin full of water, beside which sat a towel, washcloth and bar of soap. To their dismay, they discovered there was no indoor plumbing — after all, Lincoln would not have had such — which might have accounted for the low price. An outhouse stood between their cabin and the one next door; since they seemed to be the only customers that night, at least it would not be occupied by someone else, they assured each other. For light there was only a kerosene lantern, which helped them decide to make it an early night. With no curtain on the only window, which was over the counter, they could see a full moon shining down, looking for all the world like a worried old man.

As he had taken to doing, Teddy slept at the foot of their bed. Susan was amazed at how well behaved he was. "Why in the world would anybody abandon him?" she said that night as she stroked his silky fur. To which Lois could only reply, "He must have gotten separated from his people somehow. Maybe he started to chase something and got lost, and they couldn't find him. Maybe he fell out of a car. Nobody with any heart at all would leave such a lovely dog behind." "Maybe," Susan speculated, "his owners just couldn't afford to feed him any longer." That image made them both feel sad.

"No matter," Lois replied. "He belongs to us now. He'll never go hungry again."

The sun woke them early in the morning, before either felt quite like getting up. But they needed to get on the road, so get up they did. Using the counter-top cook stove to make pancakes, they enjoyed a quick breakfast, gave Teddy some canned meat and got underway. Thus far in Illinois they had met with no mishaps, encountered no dangerous people, or experienced any bad weather. In fact, it had been warm and sunny but not unbearably hot. "Must be a good omen," Susan remarked. Lois (she who had said the tire incident was a good omen) replied that she doubted it; whatever was going to happen just hadn't happened yet. Susan had to laugh at her dear friend's Eeyore-like prognostication, so untypical of her, but she kept her comments to herself. Generally she was the one who got gloomy from time to time; Lois was happy and optimistic. Susan decided all that driving was wearing her friend down.

Route 66 heading to Chicago was more populated with towns—and with traffic—than the road had been up until then. Of course, Illinois had long been settled—even though, once, it had been considered part of the vast unknown western landscape, an unexplored, mysterious wilderness. Those days were long gone; Illinois was a very civilized, settled state as far as they could tell. Of course, like the rest of America it had a chequered history: there had once been race riots in Springfield; Chicago had a nationwide reputation as gang land, and the southern half of the state was known to have had Confederate sympathies during the Civil War, leading to a significant divide between the two areas. Nonetheless, so far Illinois had not disappointed or discouraged them, and the road was paved.

They drove well past dusk on the second day, arriving weary, hungry and sore in Joliet to find a place to lay their heads. The street lights helped guide them toward a brightly lit sign that promised, enticingly, Your Home Away From Home. Too exhausted to worry about the cost, they turned Theda into the driveway and secured a room for the night. "If this was my home away from home, I'd go back to my own home in a minute," Lois muttered. The room they had taken was not much bigger than the miniature cabin where they'd slept (albeit well enough) the night before. It had a bed not quite the size of a double, with a very tired bedspread covering the mattress, a small sink, a hot plate, a coffee pot, and a bathroom with, glory of glories, a shower. ("Thank goodness for that," Susan commented.) No table or chair, nothing to set their belongings on. But it was only $1.50 a night, so it would do.

By this time Susan was yearning for her own comfortable bed, her private room, and her quiet life at the library. Quick wash-ups at the sink were simply not the same as a warm shower to make one feel scrubbed clean. She felt unwashed, displaced and grumpy, but she said nothing to Lois, not wanting to dampen her friend's spirits. After all, they hadn't even gotten to Chicago yet. Unbeknownst to her, Lois was having similar yearnings for the life she had so blithely left behind. "Traveling," she remarked as they heated up yet another can of beans for supper, "sure helps you appreciate the comforts of home." Susan nodded fervently. "Indeed it does." Neither dared go any further with that conversation, so they descended into a brief discussion of getting to Chicago in the morning.

"Oh, dear; I have no clean panties left," Susan said as she began to unpack her pajamas. "Only a pair for tomorrow. And my brassiere really needs washing out." Lois began rummaging through her duffle bag. "Oops! Neither do I. Well, we just have to wash our things in that sink and hang them up to dry overnight." Since they'd stopped camping they had not found another place to do laundry such as was available in some campgrounds.

But to their dismay, when they arose in the morning the laundry they'd draped over the bedstead and the shower rod was still quite damp. They could not wait for it to dry. What to do? Lois came up with a wild idea. "Let's hang it in the bed of the truck," she suggested.

"How can we do that?"

"We'll string a rope from the front to the back and hang our dainties on it. They're sure to get dry before we get to Chicago." Not having any better ideas, Susan went along with the extraordinary suggestion and rigged the rope up in the truck bed. They secured their underthings with clothespins (except for Susan's brassiere, which she had to wear damp, it being the only one she had) and took off for the big city.

Thus did they make their way into Chicago, their underwear waving majestically in the breeze as they rode along. First stop was for relief—for themselves and for Teddy. They found a gas station on the edge of town which offered facilities; while one used them, the other walked around with Teddy, who, gentleman that he was, chose a private spot to do his business. He walked slowly, nose to the ground, ears down. "We have to find a place that takes pets when we get home," Susan said as she climbed back into the truck. "We have to find our way around this city first," Lois replied. For the first time since they embarked on the trip, Susan thought Lois looked nervous when she got back behind the wheel. True, the traffic was formidable, the streets were narrow and parking spaces seemed to be at a premium. They had come this far, though; now was not the time for timidity. Susan found time to make a note in her journal when they stopped at the edge of the city to determine their direction.

I am excited to be in Chicago at last even if we did arrive with our undies on display. People probably got a good laugh watching us drive by. No harm in that; people need to find things to laugh about these days. My word; I would never have made such a comment before this trip! I would be crimson with embarrassment. We'll never see these people again, though, and they have no idea who we are. So I can laugh about it.

Chapter Thirteen—Chicago at Last

The atmosphere in Chicago was startlingly different from the city where they lived. For one, it was much noisier—lots of honking, shouting, rattling and banging of metal objects. It was not as clean as Denver either; the sidewalks had not been swept recently (they were reminded of how residents in the Capitol Hill area of Denver swept their stoops every morning), and a variety of smells, some appealing, some not, assailed them, seeping into the truck. Teddy's nose twitched; the assault on his sense of smell was probably overwhelming. He didn't bark or get restless; he just sniffed and sniffed.

Traffic was heavy; the air seemed thick and somewhat oppressive. And the city appeared endless, stretching beyond the horizon in every direction. Susan the librarian had learned everything she could about Chicago before they left. For one, she knew they were entering on the South Side. (Oddly, there were only three Sides, South, North and West.) This city appeared to be clusters of smaller cities clumped together and called Chicago, for each part of it was distinct and different from the others. The South Side, said to be rather rundown, gave an impression of indifference. It was clearly multi-cultural, for they saw people of many different ethnicities on the sidewalks and stoops.

"It certainly is colorful," Susan commented. "But I wonder how we'll ever get any sleep. It is so noisy!"

"Let's find a place to stay first, then we can decide what to do." Lois was gripping the steering wheel with grim determination, dodging around vehicles parked, with no apparent intention of moving any time soon, in the middle of the street; avoiding oncoming traffic on narrow streets, and watching intently for pedestrians, who seemed to have no interest in looking out for cars. Most of them walked with their heads down, intent on attaining some unknown destination and undeterred by obstacles in their path such as cars. Lois muttered under her breath.

"Why did we want to come to Chicago?" she said after a particularly trying maneuver. "To see the sights," Susan responded. "To have new experiences before we settle down." Lois only gritted her teeth. "Keep an eye peeled for a motel with a 'Vacant' sign." Susan didn't see any motels like the ones where they had stayed on the road, but she saw several hotels, some rather seedy-looking. They turned a corner off the main drag and found themselves, within a few blocks, in a different world of two- and three-story houses, attached to each other but distinctive in décor, with little gardens in front, trees here and there, and clear sidewalks; the stoops, too, had been swept clean. People strolled along past the buildings — a young mother pushing a baby carriage, two youths sporting colorful shirts and vests (Lois declared them cocky), men in suits and ties and fedoras, women bustling along looking purposeful. Here and there, an older man or woman sat on a stoop, looking — just looking. Susan could have watched the people parade for hours.

"Maybe we can find something around here." Lois looked around her hopefully. "In fact…" She pulled over to the curb and parked. Hopping out of the truck, she walked up to a woman (middle-aged, with gray hair, medium height) who appeared purposeful but not in too much of a hurry.

"Excuse me," she said. "We're from out of town." She gestured at Susan sitting in the truck. "We're looking for a clean, safe, inexpensive place to spend a few nights. Do you have any suggestions? Oh, and we have a small dog."

Somewhat taken aback judging by her expression, the woman paused and tilted her head. "Three blocks west of here there's the Georgian Hotel. It's very nice, clean, and reasonable. I'm not sure about the dog, but you know, so many hotels have closed, and it's still open, so they might be just glad to have you anyway."

Lois held out her hand. "Lois Parker, from Denver," she said. The hand was met by the stranger's. "Helen Perry from Boston," she replied. "My sister, Carolyn, and I moved here to be with our brother. The three of us are all the family that's left now."

"How is it for you here? Is it better than Boston?"

"Carolyn found a job with an insurance company as a secretary, and Donald works at the stockyards. So far, I have not found employment." Her Boston accent was crisp, defined. Lois smiled and thanked Miss Perry. "I wish you luck with your job hunt." Helen Perry nodded and walked on. As she walked away, Lois could see that her shoes were worn down at the heels, her hose had been mended a few times, and her hat was frayed at the edges. Hard times. Again, how Lois wished she could do something to help, but there was nothing to do. A whole nation was suffering and it seemed there was nothing anyone could do. Smartly dressed though she always was, Lois herself turned collars, mended stockings and underwear and added trim to cover wear and tear on fabric. She did that for Susan too.

The Georgian proved to be charming, an intimate place with only eight rooms, pets allowed. It also proved costly at $2.50 a night, but that did include breakfast. Four rooms shared one bathroom down the hall, which meant little chance of a good soothing soak in the tub; still, that was a minor inconvenience. Given the size of the city and the noise they had encountered so far, it was surprisingly quiet inside the rectangular brick building. A man and his wife, who introduced themselves as Mr. and Mrs. Gorman, both somewhere in their forties, Susan surmised, ran the hotel and seemed very friendly and welcoming. The fee included coffee, fruit and pastries for breakfast; they were used to a light breakfast anyway, and the coffee would be a treat, no extra charge.

Lois's only worry was leaving the Ford outside, possible prey to thieves, but the owners assured her it would be safe. There was a small gang of youths, teenaged boys the owners trusted, available for hire to guard guests' vehicles and their contents overnight for only 50 cents. Mr. Gorman did suggest that they consider removing any valuable items from the back of the truck while touring around the city; their possessions would be safe in the hotel lobby, he assured them. Susan's strong intuitions about people told her that he was trustworthy and that they should take his advice, which they did. He had an enclosed area at the back of the small lobby to store guests' valuables. Not wanting to take any chances, they stowed everything there, for all of it was valuable in their eyes. It took a while to unload Theda, but doing so gave them peace of mind.

Chicago, they quickly saw, was a city built around water. Not only was it on the shore of Lake Michigan; the Chicago River ran right through the center of town. It was heavily used for transporting goods; several bridges crossed it. Other rivers intersected the town as well, the Des Plaines and the Calumet. There was water, water everywhere. On the banks of the rivers they saw fishermen casting off into the water, though they never saw anyone catch anything. All of the river water looked rather murky, unlike the Platte which rushed through the center of Denver, its clear water sparkling in the sunshine.

Not that there was a lot of sun in Chicago. At least while they were in the city, clouds dominated, with the sun peeking through from time to time. It leant a rather gloomy aspect to the atmosphere of the metropolis. Lois and Susan were accustomed to sunshine. Most days in Denver, the sun shone the better part of the day. Both of them tended to grow a bit gloomy when the sun disappeared for a few days, as it did from time to time. But it seemed to them that in Chicago, the sun was a sometime visitor only.

"Of course, we can't really judge," Susan reminded Lois. "We're only here for a short time. Maybe it's sunny a lot more than it is right now."

"Maybe," Lois acknowledged, "but it's sure not sunny right now."

It wasn't that the clouds were menacing, holding rain that might come down any minute. They were not dark like the thunderclouds that often showed up on summer afternoons at home. They were just gray, wispy clouds, high in the sky, hanging there with no particular purpose either one of them could discern. Just clouds, obscuring the sun.

Looking back later, they chuckled when reminiscing about their time in Chicago, vaunted haunt of the mob, that their time there had been the least thrilling part of the entire trip. That's not to say there weren't memorable sights to enjoy: Susan was awed by the majesty of the Carnegie, outside and in. Roaming the stacks, she discovered new Dewey designations she had never encountered before and duly noted them in her journal. The sheer volume of books was almost overwhelming. The silence was reverential, patrons scurrying about making as little noise as humanly possible or sitting at tables reading intently. Her little county library could have fitted into that magnificent edifice at least five times over; she thought it must take a large staff to manage all those volumes and indeed she did see several official-looking people walking around with books and a purposeful look. The library was crowded with patrons, who read newspapers, perused magazines, selected books or studied reference works, taking notes meticulously. She loved the look, the smell, the feel of the place and could have stayed there all day, but Lois was outside walking around with Teddy and they still had sights Lois wanted to see, so Susan reluctantly left. Lois took several shots of the library's exterior.

Teddy was in transports of delight over the explosion of odors he encountered. He spent his time outdoors industriously sniffing the ground, apparently smelling all kinds of new scents and absorbed in his discoveries. The mere human noses belonging to his people could identify some of the myriad smells in the air—automobile exhaust, humidity, water, cooking food, and a few others they could not quite pin down. But they knew Teddy could distinguish hundreds more. To the two travelers, the air seemed far heavier than in Denver, more redolent of a mixture of smells, most of them not particularly pleasant. They were accustomed to the agricultural smells pervasive around Denver at certain times of the year—harvested crops being transported, as well as cattle and their leavings passing through—and to other city smells like autos, but wind whistling down from the mountains frequently cleansed the air. In Chicago, it seemed, the smells never dissipated but hung like mist, permeating everything.

The sight best remembered by them both, though, was the lake, which stretched into infinity or so it appeared, the water rippling, tickling the shore. Theda tickety-tocked along the road beside the great body of water. She took her sweet time, oblivious to the heavier, faster vehicles behind, in front, and coming toward her. Soon they found a beach near the aquarium, crowded with sunbathers and swimmers on that early-summer day. Lois was able to tuck Theda, who was after all rather small, into a tight parking space so they could get out and poke around a bit. Bathing costumes, they noted, had certainly improved since their childhoods, when women were almost entirely covered before entering the water, a condition that severely inhibited swimming. Like Susan at the library, Lois could have stayed there all day. She had never seen such a vast body of water before; she was astounded. None of the mountain lakes in Colorado came anywhere close to the size of Lake Michigan. She took pictures from all angles while Susan strolled around with Teddy, who was having a glorious time sniffing the air and the ground.

But just seeing it proved not to be enough. Fully clothed people were wading in the water, minus shoes and stockings. Lois and Susan called on their bravado and decided to do the same. Lois worried about their abandoning their boots ashore, but Susan took care of that; finding a kindly-looking older Negro woman who sat serenely on a bench watching the people around her, Susan asked her to keep an eye on their things and on Teddy (who would not venture close to the water; they both wondered why but were never to know). The woman, who wore a faded-blue, loose print dress with buttons down the front and a broad-brimmed canvas hat, wreathed her wrinkled face into a smile and said of course she would do that, and was there anything else she could do? Susan told her that when they came back out, they would like to buy her an ice cream cone. She said she would love a strawberry one.

111

To them it felt oppressively hot; the heat, similar to what they had encountered most of the way, was cloying. Although a slight breeze came off the lake, nothing seemed to relieve the weighty, moist heat that clung to their clothes and caused them to perspire profusely. So the water was especially tempting.

They took off their shoes and stockings, rolled up their pant legs, and waded in. The water was cold but not unbearably so; however, their tender feet were not prepared for the gravelly bottom of the lake by the shore. But oh! It felt so good. Gentle waves lapped at their ankles; the sun was shining, and people looked happy and carefree, at least in that moment. Laughter and light chatter floated around. From time to time a slight breeze stirred the muggy air. Pure bliss and blessed forgetfulness, for a short while anyway.

When they came back to the shore the woman, who said her name was Mabel, was sitting beside their stockings and boots and from the voluminous pocketbook on her lap produced a small towel which she offered to them for wiping off their feet. Lois went off in search of an ice cream stand and soon found one. She bought three strawberry cones, the largest size they had, which they all licked luxuriously; Teddy, of course, got the last bites of Lois's and Susan's cones, a reward for waiting patiently by the bench while his people went into the water. He had been carefully tended by Mabel and clearly enjoyed his treat. They heaped thanks on her, and she smiled and replied that she'd been only too glad to help. It got a little boring, she acknowledged, sitting here all day, but she didn't reveal why she did that. Had they been in possession of any extra money, Lois would have slipped her some. But their funds were running low. Mabel, patiently sitting on a bench by the beach all day long, became another mystery for Susan's journal. But Lois and Susan created stories about her: perhaps the lake had taken someone she had loved who'd never been found, and she was waiting, hoping, for his return. Or she might have once worked on a ship of the lake and was reminiscing about those better days…

A memorable day if ever there had been one, Susan and Lois agreed that night as they prepared for bed. (Twin beds, a treat for Susan.)

Undoubtedly the most challenging aspect of Chicago was the traffic, more than they had ever seen in Denver or even the bigger metropolis of St. Louis. Lois used every one of her skills and learned some new maneuvers while dealing with vehicles of all types and sizes. Some drivers were courteous; most were in a hurry and couldn't take time to be polite. It seemed that there was an enormous amount of honking (not infrequently accompanied by loud swearing) going on all the time; sometimes, Lois joined the cacophony. Theda's horn made a particularly satisfying honk, deep but sharp. Though Lois (heroically, in Susan's eyes) avoided having an actual collision, they had several heart-stopping near misses.

They continued along the lake shore road the next day to visit Navy Pier, a sight not to miss, they'd been told. It was indeed a wonder to behold. They walked all the way to the end of it, more than 3,000 feet, and peered at the vastness beyond: to the north, nothing but water, boats and big ships melded into the horizon. People milled about, taking in the view. Some were picnicking. Children were riding the carousel, their high, childish laughter ringing out through the air. Susan's heart filled with joy. She basked in the lightness of simply being.

They admired the storied Palmer Hotel, went to the Art Institute and Shedd Aquarium, and window-shopped at Marshall Fields, Lois admiring the latest styles, which had not yet made their way to Denver. The hotel was breathtakingly magnificent, ornate and dignified; guests glided around on plush carpets, noise was muted, and bellhops helped people with their luggage. It surprised them both that anyone could afford to stay there in the midst of the Depression, yet the place gave every impression of being popular. They saw exotic cars in the parking area to the side of the building. In the lobby, women in expensive clothes and elegant hats and men with shiny, tailored suits sat or stood drinking cocktails near the bar (purchasing what appeared to be nonalcoholic drinks, but who knew what was actually in them?).

They all seemed to be smoking; the women used long cigarette holders and seldom puffed on their cigarettes, just holding them at the prescribed angle to one side; the men mostly had cigars, which smelled unpleasant, Lois commented in a low-voiced aside. They both felt out of place in their everyday, rather grubby traveling pants and shirts and did not stay long. (Susan wondered whether there was a speakeasy for the really hard stuff. With guests like these, she supposed there was, but one no doubt had to know the magic words to get in. Not that she wanted to; it was just her natural curiosity surfacing as it so often did. Lois had been told about the Riviera Restaurant where those in the know walked through the pantry to rooms where they could buy mixed drinks; it was rumored that Al Capone supplied the whiskey and beer. Dumb waiters delivered meals made in a basement kitchen for those who chose to dine. Adventurous though these intrepid travelers were, they had decided not to include it on their itinerary—far too close to the mob activities the city was famous for.)

They peeked into the Drake Hotel too, admiring the famed Gold Coast room where, it was rumored, cocktails were readily available despite Prohibition; everyone knew it and no one objected, least of all the police. Of course, in gangland Chicago, who worried about Prohibition? They couldn't help gawking at the ornate décor. (Rumor also had it that, if one were very fortunate, sightings of such luminaries as Charles and Anne Lindbergh or one of the Gershwins might occur. No such luck for them—of course, it was daytime, so what could they expect? People like that probably didn't even get out of bed before noon and stayed up most of the night. So they'd heard.)

At the Art Institute they saw paintings so vivid and lifelike it seemed they might walk right off the walls—the work of masters, unmatched by ordinary artists. The paintings took their breath away. Both of them could have lingered much longer. Lois bought several postcards of paintings. At the aquarium they encountered sea creatures they had never heard of before, curiosities of all shapes and sizes. Neither had ever been to the ocean; both, after seeing the aquarium's inhabitants, wanted to. Marshall Fields was a multi-storied wonder, offering goods for every facet of life. It had elevators that moved customers from floor to floor and a shop where they could get a cup of coffee and a pastry—even, if they were so inclined, a sandwich. Unable to resist temptation, they treated themselves to a shared apple turnover served with warm cream, and some of the best coffee, dark and rich, that either of them had ever enjoyed.

They worried about tying Teddy outside, but no one snatched him. (Lois theorized that he growled and bared his teeth if anyone came too close, besides which, who wanted an extra mouth to feed in these times?) As far as they knew and somewhat to their disappointment, they did not see a single gangster (from a safe distance, of course), although they weren't entirely sure they would know one if they did. There were uniformed policemen around, though, most places they went. All large men, these law enforcement officers had grim, determined looks and rather fierce eyes. They had truncheons on their belts and walked with their shoulders back, their heads high. Susan felt a frisson of fear when one passed by, but she did not feel they would do her or Lois harm. Neither was she certain they would protect them, however.

Bread lines appeared here and there, long ones, and on every corner there seemed to be someone seeking a handout—mostly men in ragged clothing, but sometimes fairly young, grubby children with a parent nearby while the child, with an appealing expression, held out a tin cup. Not all of their interactions with others were friendly or cheerful, although by in large people were not openly rude. But it was certainly not like Denver, where strangers often exchanged a few words of greeting as they passed each other on the street. To Lois and Susan, people in Chicago came across as distant—not hostile, just indifferent or preoccupied.

They did encounter a few undeniably rude individuals. One, a short, stout man who accidentally (so it appeared, anyway) bumped Lois's arm grumbled at her nastily to get out of his way. Another, a young woman selling rather withered apples at a corner stall, practically snarled at them when they walked right on without stopping to buy one from her. Susan declined to record in her journal the ugly words the woman spat at them.

Taking offense at the responses of others seemed petty. People

115

in general did not appear to be happy during these hard economic times; almost everyone was struggling to make ends meet. So unpleasant interactions with others were not entirely outside of what could be considered normal in America in 1932. They had both had similar encounters from time to time in Denver. But sometimes enough is enough. When a beggar stepped right in front of them as they were walking down the street and demanded money, they both shook their heads and moved around him carefully. He walked off muttering, "Bitches." That was too much for Lois. She turned around and caught up with him, took hold of his right arm, and said, in her sternest tone, "Apologize for what you called us. And if you don't, our dog would love to have a taste of your leg."

The man looked up at her, looked down at Teddy's obligingly bared teeth, and said through gritted teeth, "Sorry." Lois let go of his arm and stalked away. She tamped down her anger as they walked; Susan could see her friend visibly calming herself. "No one speaks of us that way, Sue. No one." Then she said no more on the subject. Somehow Susan was reassured by the incident. It put her in mind of the way they stood up to that small-minded sheriff. They could, did, and would take care of themselves.

Food was interesting in Chicago. People sold sandwiches, hot dogs and sausages right on the street for very low prices — 10 cents for a hot dog with a bun, 15 cents for a sausage roll. In small parks here and there they found water fountains. The water was tepid but tasted all right. (Not as good as Denver water, of course.)

The sidewalk offerings were sufficient to their needs; the sausages were actually quite filling and tasty. Teddy liked them, too. For their evening meal they bought hot baked potatoes and ate them in the lobby of their hotel. The manager very kindly brought them complementary sarsaparilla to drink. He bottled it himself, he told them. There was no possibility either of them would venture out into the city after dark; they returned to the hotel as the sun was setting with every intention of staying there. Tired as they were, more touring in the evening didn't appeal to them in any case.

The heat did not abate at night, just as had been the case the farther east they went. The air remained muggy, almost suffocating at times. So much for pajamas; they both slept in their under things without a blanket, just a sheet for modesty (in case someone came into the room unexpectedly, although the door was locked). Teddy curled up on the floor between their beds, panting a bit. Their room in the hotel was relatively cool, being on the second floor at the back of the stone building with a huge shade tree right outside the window, and a fan in the window made a valiant effort to stave off the worst of the heat. Even so, they were hot. "It's still early in June, not even officially summer," Lois remarked on their first evening in the hotel. "How in the world do people stand it in the middle of the summer when it gets really, really hot?"

Standing in front of the fan in her under things, the legs of her panties blowing in the breeze, Susan could only shake her head in wonder. "I will never complain about the heat at home again," she replied. They both know that was an impossible pledge to keep— they would and did complain when it got hot in Denver—but at that moment, Susan really meant what she said. Her garments clung to her skin, slick with sweat, and her hair stuck to her scalp.

Lois thought it was the heat she would remember most. In the big buildings, ceiling fans moved slowly to circulate the air, but they didn't help all that much. Near the lake there was often a breeze, but farther inshore the atmosphere was thick with heat that seemed to shimmer off the sidewalks. Mixed with the assorted odors that wafted around, they found the environment somewhat depressing. On their second day in the city, they were bombarded by a torrential rainstorm, whereupon they discovered one important item they had indeed neglected to bring—umbrellas. With the drought in Colorado, it had never occurred to them that it might actually rain where they were going. They took shelter under a canopy in front of a store, waiting for it to stop, but it seemed to go on for a long time. Lightning flashed, thunder crashed, and Teddy leaned hard against Susan's legs, trembling. When the rain stopped at last, they were dismayed to discover that the rain didn't cool things down one bit; it

117

just soaked everything in sight.

By the end of that day they were foot sore, satiated, weary and ready to head homeward. All in all, they agreed, it had been a rewarding destination. They would never forget the sights they had seen, and they had wonderful stories to tell their friends when they returned home.

If L had not come up with the idea of taking a road trip I would never have seen such splendid sights. I shall never forget the Carnegie, and the lake—words fail me. The sight of it makes me want to see an ocean. Perhaps we will get to California one day. More wonders to take in. I am so happy that she took the bull by the horns, so to speak. On my own, I no doubt would have sold Theda (she would have missed all this adventure too; how sad!). It would never have occurred to me to take her on a trip. Dear L, how I love and cherish her. It was my lucky day when she came into my life. With Mama, Papa and Richard gone, she is my family. L says the same of me, although she has blood relations. We are as close as sisters. Still, I have yet to tell her that I am in love. Is it to be unrequited love? I wish I knew.

Road Trip

Chapter Fourteen—Homeward Bound

The sight of the big city becoming smaller behind them was heartening. "I'm glad we went there even if was hot and stuffy," Susan declared as they headed south again. Lois nodded, once more intent on dealing with the traffic. The farther away from Chicago they went, the less traffic there was, and in a few hours she visibly relaxed at the wheel. Spotting a service station, she pulled over for gas and a restroom visit—and, of course, relief for the ever-patient Teddy.

What wondrous sights they were bringing home with them, to be shared and remembered: They had seen Hoovervilles and bread lines and beggars and hoboes. They had stood on the shore of Lake Michigan and seen no end to the water, and they had experienced the water for themselves. Susan had spent precious time at the Carnegie. They had admired magnificent structures and creative roadside buildings. They had walked to the end of the Navy Pier and seen amazing creatures at the aquarium. They had viewed priceless, timeless art by masters. They had marvelous stories to tell upon their return. Most of all, they had met remarkable people in extraordinary circumstances. Who could have asked for more?

Neither of them expected further excitement on the way home, after all that had happened on the northbound trip. They told each other it would be smooth going all the way back to Denver—they knew the roads, having come that way; they knew some people, and they knew where to stay. They had helped deliver a baby, been invited into the homes of strangers, found and adopted a stray dog, watched a man die in front of them and faced down an angry sheriff, fed a hungry man, slept in their tent and heard coyotes howl, and cooked over an open fire. A lifetime of adventure in such a short time—what else could possibly happen? Route 66 was familiar, the sun was shining, fluffy white clouds floated by, the road was paved and smooth. Life was good.

Ah, the optimism of the young...

ROUND THE CORNER/ LICKITY SPLIT/ BEAUTIFUL CAR/ WASN'T IT? / BURMA SHAVE

And oh, yes, Susan was getting quite a collection of Burma Shave signs along the way.

Dixie Trucker's Home in McLean was a surprise. Touted as one of the first such places in the country, the store and café catered to long-haul truckers, who clearly appreciated the place as evidenced by the roomful of burly drivers; mostly large, bearded men, they typically wore denim pants and checkered shirts, often accompanied by colorful suspenders and topped by newsboy hats rather than the fedoras sported by businessmen. They were by in large loud and raucous, and the building reeked with cigarette and cigar smoke. Susan and Lois did not linger long, but Lois did manage to surreptitiously get a couple of photographs of them and of some of the trucks, which were carrying all manner of goods including livestock. When the two friends entered the café, they were met with catcalls and whistles. Arm in arm, they took a seat in a booth and ignored the crudities, but admittedly they drank their coffee and ate their hot dogs pretty quickly then scooted back out to the safety of the flivver, which Teddy was diligently guarding. Sheer curiosity, plus the chance of another story to tell when they got home again, had brought them into the café, but they had not expected quite such a reception nor realized they would be the only women for miles around (except for the waitresses, of course, who gave as good as they got).

Aside from Dixie's, on the first day homeward-bound nothing

unusual occurred, with the slight exception of Teddy almost getting sprayed by a skunk. They had stopped to picnic beside the road and Teddy had done his usual exploring nearby. He was fine there without his leash, or so they thought. Then the fat striped creature waddled out of the bushes a few feet away and came toward them, tail held high. "Skunk!" cried Susan, familiar with those unloved animals. Lois reached out and snatched up Teddy just as the skunk was preparing to let loose its noxious odor. Teddy buried his head under Lois's arm and sat down in the truck as they sped away. To their relief, the skunk turned around and left without perfuming the air. Lois even got a photo of the creature retreating.

As Chicago faded into the distance, Susan began to notice the sounds of country life—birds calling, vegetation rustling as small creatures moved through it, trees sighing in the intermittent breeze. Accompanied by the rhythmic ticking of Theda trundling along the road, the gentle noises were like music, a symphony she had not heard since they entered the city. She basked in the contrast to all that constant metropolitan racket. For a moment, she was back at the farm, the symphony expanded by the murmuring of the cows, the restless movement of the plow horse's feet in the barn, clucking chickens and buzzing bees. Not all at once, of course; each orchestral section had its own turn in the spotlight. She blinked away a few tears and looked around her—she was not in the farmyard with her family nearby but in a 1927 Model T Ford pickup with her best friend, Lois, heading for home on a bright blue summer day.

"How wonderfully quiet it is," she commented to Lois, who nodded her agreement but did not reply.

"Chicago is so much noisier than Denver," she added. "More traffic, more people, more things happening. I don't think I could bear to live in such a busy place."

"I've always liked the city noises," Lois replied after a thoughtful moment. "But I agree; Chicago is too much for me." They fell into a reflective silence, stopping when they found a suitable motel (boring name and style but quiet and clean) to spend the night, having mutually agreed to avoid camping out if at all possible, and all three of them enjoyed a peaceful night's rest even though they did have to sneak Teddy in. Such a dog—he never uttered a peep once inside their cabin.

Susan was getting concerned about their funds. Lois was paying for motels every night, and the hotel in Chicago, plus food and protection for their truck, had been costly. They had bought some food and been given some along the way. Their supplies in the truck were holding up fairly well. Still, they were feeding Teddy along with themselves. "How is the money holding out?" she asked when they stopped for a picnic lunch of peanut butter with crackers and cold canned beans. Rather meager fare for Teddy, Susan lamented, but he did not seem to mind, downing the offering as soon as it was set before him.

"We have enough to get us home, but there won't be any left over," was the reply.

"So we need to be really careful from now on?"

"Yes, I think so. We might need to camp again, though." She grimaced at the prospect. "I know it was my idea. It sounded romantic, and kind of daring, and I thought…Well, if we have to, we will. Coyotes or no coyotes."

"We won't always be so far from a town," Susan pointed out. "We might be able to camp close to civilization." Lois merely nodded, distracted by her memory of the howling canines. They cleaned up from the picnic and got back on the road. The landscape looked much the same, though the heat had gotten more intense, appearing in waves just above the surface, invisible yet perceivable in a way neither had ever seen in Colorado. Cows lay down, tails swishing to keep away the flies. Even the birds were lethargic, though they did see a large hawk sweep up some kind of fair-sized rodent and carry it off. No breeze stirred the tree leaves; the sun was unhindered by a single cloud.

Theda was sluggish, too. As they pulled away from the picnic spot she began to balk from time to time, shuddering and then lurching forward. Finally Lois pulled off, got out, and opened the hood. Lois and Susan peered anxiously at the engine. Well, Lois was peering;

Susan, even on tiptoes, could not see a thing. She'd have had to climb onto the bumper to discover what was happening to the engine.

"I have no idea in the world what I am looking at," Lois told Susan. "No idea at all." Both realized at that moment that they had expected Theda to be trouble-free on the trip, with no mechanical problems, for neither was knowledgeable about car engines; plus, they had no tools to repair engines in any case. Clearly, however, Theda had no plans to move forward any time soon. So much for thinking they would have an uneventful trip home. By Susan's father's pocket watch it was around 2 p.m.; the heat would linger for several more hours before the slight cooldown after sunset. Lois straightened up. "I guess I'll have to go for help. My legs are longer than yours, so I can get to the next town faster than you could. You and Teddy stay here and guard our stuff." Susan nodded dejectedly and perched on the running board, Teddy by her side. Lois set off southward along the side of the road, her head full of worry about how in the world they could pay for repairs to the car. There simply was not one penny to spare.

She had not gone far, though, when another Model T pickup came along on the other side of the road. The driver parked, got out, and walked over to Lois. "Problems, miss?" he said. "I saw your truck a ways back there." Lois nodded. "Our truck just stalled, and it won't start. I'm going to the next town to get some help." She started to walk again, having no intention of asking for—or accepting—a ride from a strange man. The man was going north, in any case. He stepped up beside her. "Owen Anderton. I have a farm a couple miles north. Can I take a look at your truck? Might be I know what's wrong with it. As you can see, I have one just like it." Lois set aside her hesitation and hopped into his truck; he'd said he was a farmer, and Susan claimed farmers were well-intentioned people... As he turned his truck around and headed back toward theirs, she studied his profile.

Owen Anderton certainly wasn't Hollywood handsome. His forehead was too high; his eyebrows jutted out slightly over his eyes; a brown beard (sans mustache), albeit neatly trimmed, concealed his prominent chin. His nose seemed a little too large for his square face, and his cheeks were sharply peaked. In fact, he reminded her in a way of Abraham Lincoln. Of average height, she guessed five foot eight or nine inches, he was solid and muscular—his muscles seemed to ripple even when he was not moving. On the other hand, his light brown hair, tinged with blond highlights, lay upon his head in enviable waves; his impossibly, unfairly long eyelashes fringed intelligent, piercing blue eyes; his cheeks were lightly tinged with healthy color, and his half smile was warm and genuine. His teeth were white and even. His frame, though stocky, was nonetheless lean and firm. Lois took all that in with unexpected pleasure.

When they got back to Theda he bent under the hood, went back to his truck to get a tool, then made some motions mysterious to both of them and straightened up again. "Just some wires that got jarred loose," he told them. "Try it now." Obligingly, Lois got behind the wheel. (Had she been the type, she might have said a quick prayer, but that was not in her nature.) She turned on the ignition and wiped her brow with relief when Theda started up quite readily. Hopping back out again, she walked over to Owen Anderton and held out her hand, not minding at all that his was grubby with engine grime. "We are so grateful to you, and so glad you came along when you did." He smiled back at her, a blinding smile that lit up his whole face. Why, he was indeed Hollywood handsome, she decided. With a smile like that, he could take film-land by storm.

Susan gave her a little poke in the ribs. "He's talking to us," she whispered. "Oh," Lois said. "Sorry. I was just trying to think how we could repay you. We don't have much money, but would you like a box of cookies?" He gave her a puzzled look. "Why on earth would I want money, or cookies for that matter?" he replied. "I was just helping out a couple of stranded travelers. It's what any decent folks would do." He paused, then wiped his brow with a red-checkered kerchief that had hung loosely around his neck. "It surely is hot. Would you ladies like to come up the farm for some ice tea?"

(Curious, Susan thought, how everyone they'd met on the way called it 'ice tea' not 'iced tea.') She nudged Lois again, and they both nodded their agreement. Cold tea was simply too tempting to resist—and so, for Lois, was Owen Anderton. If he turned out to be a dangerous man luring them into his home to do them harm, she would take the chance. Lois turned the truck around and followed Owen to his farm, which was as he'd promised just a short way up the road. So once again they found themselves bumping along a rutted dirt road to a stranger's farmhouse, uncertain of what they would encounter. But Susan had seen the look in Lois's eyes when they met Owen Anderton; if they had not accepted his invitation, Lois might have kicked Susan into kingdom come. Well, not really, but she would have been very, very unhappy.

The house was a white, square, two-story box. On the front porch sat two rocking chairs along with a porch swing. A small table covered with a doily perched between the rockers. On one side in front of the porch was a bed of pink and red roses, lovingly tended; on the other side, geraniums bloomed in the sun. The front door, beautifully carved wood, opened as they approached. Owen gestured for them to come in. Holding the door open stood one of the tiniest people either of them had ever come across. "And I thought I was short" flashed through Susan's mind. For the woman could not have been even five feet tall, whereas Susan was five feet three inches high. Nor was the woman rotund. She could hardly have weighed 100 pounds, Susan thought. The woman stood almost in the doorway of a cavernous kitchen which had a table with a checkered cloth in the middle, chairs around it, and a curtained window over the sink.

"This is my Aunt Frances," said Owen. To the small woman he said, "Auntie, meet Lois Parker and Susan Mayfield. Oh, and Teddy." (Teddy had become their harbinger. Had he reacted badly to Owen, the two women would have skedaddled. But the little dog sniffed Owen's feet and wagged his tail vigorously. Owen passed muster.)

To Lois and Susan Owen said, "Come on into the parlor." In the rather formal parlor they sat down on matching horsehair wing chairs on either side of a large, apparently well used fireplace, on the mantel of which was an array of sepia photographs. "My family," said Owen, pointing at the pictures. "My grandparents and their siblings. Auntie is my father's sister." (He pronounced it the Eastern way, "awnty," Susan noted.) Teddy planted himself firmly between his two people.

"Lovely," murmured Lois, who was usually the talkative one. She raised an eyebrow at Susan, who took the hint: "Did they farm here, then?"

"Since 1863. My grandfather came west from Virginia to avoid being drafted into the Confederate army. He hated slavery and refused to fight to defend it. They homesteaded here—southern Illinois was still lightly populated then—and built the house, plank by plank. My father took over when they died, and he would be here still if he hadn't been caught by the influenza epidemic." Lois and Susan both nodded soberly. They had each lost friends during that terrible post-war time, young people who were upright and vibrant one day, dead the next, and each considered herself extremely fortunate to have escaped the epidemic. It was a searing memory. The silence of recollection filled the room for a time—until Aunt Frances bustled in with a tray of cold tea and plump cookies. "Oatmeal," she pronounced as she set down the tray. "Good for what ails you." Too polite to beg, Teddy merely looked at each of his persons, a pleading look which garnered him a couple of cookies. "Good for you," Susan whispered in his ear, "especially the raisins."

While her guests were helping themselves, Aunt Frances gave Owen an affectionate look. "When the 'flu took Lester, my brother, and then Lavinia, Owen's mother, that left me. An old maid, you know. Alone on the farm. So this good man"—she pointed at Owen—"quit his teaching job at Kansas State and came here to help me out. Bless his heart."

"What did you teach?" Lois asked, leaning forward eagerly. "History—world history, mostly, but with a small department I sometimes taught American history as well," he replied.

"I think you would have been a very good teacher," Lois replied. Susan noted a perceptible blush on her friend's cheeks. "I would have liked to take a class from you."

Owen smiled. "I might have been," he said. "I wanted to be. But my heart was really at the farm. I went to college because my father wanted me to be the first in our family to get a degree. Then I got hired at Kansas State right out of graduate school. But teaching didn't come easy to me. I like history, but I wasn't that good at making it interesting. I majored in it because I didn't know what else to study. And I hated to assign grades. Plus, the pay was dismal to put it kindly. I had to live in a rooming house with several other professors, all of us poor as church mice. Keeping order in the classroom was a challenge for me, too; my colleagues said I was too soft-hearted. So when Auntie wrote to me, I finished out the semester and came as soon as I could. I'm very happy here."

Susan could picture Lois's thoughts as she abandoned the number one item on her list for the ideal husband, that he be taller than she. Owen was perhaps two inches shorter than Lois. But oh, was he right for her in so many other ways. His speech was intelligent and precise, his manner was attentive and polite, he was kind and generous, and he was clearly fond of his elderly relative. He was good to look at, too. A good man, all around. The powerful attraction Lois was feeling was almost palpable to Susan and put her in mind of the way she had reacted to meeting Ravi, which led her to realize that Lois already knew Susan was also in love.

They enjoyed relaxing and chatting in the cool, sunlit parlor, but they knew they had to be on their way soon in order to find a good camping spot. Susan rose first, followed reluctantly by Lois. "Heading south again, where would we find a good place to camp?" she asked as they moved toward the door. At which point Auntie stepped in front of her. "Camp? You'll do no such thing. You ladies can spend the night right here, under our roof. Not very often I have women around to talk to." (Where had they heard that before...) Not at all reluctantly, Lois turned back into the house. "We don't want to put you out," Susan said, making the obligatory polite protest. "You won't be putting me out, not at all. The bed's all made up, dinner will be ready after a bit, and Owen can stow your things so the critters don't get at 'em."

127

"Critters?" Lois looked uneasy.

"Raccoons, mostly. Sometimes possums. They like to rummage around in things. Owen'll put your truck in the barn, next to his, and it'll be fine. He locks it up tight. Now sit yourselves down again and rest a spell."

So they did.

It was late afternoon by that time, and they were weary. A night's sleep in a comfortable bed was delicious to anticipate—at least Susan's thoughts went that way. Lois, on the other hand, was thunderstruck at the whirlpool of emotions roiling around inside her. She had no idea whether Owen Anderton had experienced similar sensations, and she did not intend to ask, but she was growing more and more certain of her own. How often she and Lois had laughed about love at first sight—preposterous. Silly. That only happened in books and films. It certainly wouldn't happen to her. Would it? And yet… she was sure it had happened to Susan when she encountered the handsome dark man in Kansas. She had almost felt the vibrations radiating between the two of them.

Dinner was chicken in gravy on mashed potatoes, both cooked to perfection, along with fluffy rolls, turnip greens (a new culinary experience for them both from which they emerged undecided), and raspberries with thick, rich cream to top it off, along with fragrant, freshly brewed coffee and a perfectly baked apple cake. Owen and his aunt talked some about farm matters, but most of the time they wanted to know about Denver and about their guests; they were eager to hear about life in the big city. Conversation never flagged. As Susan and Lois had lately learned, though, farmers went to bed and got up with the sun, so when the sun went down, everyone headed upstairs. Thoughtfully invited to use the facilities first, Lois and Susan hurried through their nighttime ablutions and scooted into the guest room where they had been placed. It was a homey room with country charm: frilled, flowered curtains at the windows, the ubiquitous quilt on the bed, crocheted pillow cases, doilies on the dresser and bedside tables (one on each side). Lois speculated that this had probably been Owen's parents' room. The bed, slightly larger and longer than a regular double, was comfortable and roomier than others they had shared. Sleep came easily; morning came too soon for Lois's pleasure. For on that day they simply had to move on.

Thus, after once again partaking of a hearty country breakfast (scrambled eggs cooked just right, toasted fresh-baked wheat bread, plump sausages and more aromatic, delicious coffee), they said their thanks and goodbyes. Did Lois's eyes linger too long, too longingly, on Owen as they parted? Did Owen's eyes reciprocate? Susan was not sure.

Lois is in love. My, oh my, is she in love. But what can she do about it? He lives on a farm in Illinois; she lives in Denver. She is a city girl. He is definitely not a city fellow. What a dilemma. If they were to marry, where would they live? I could not bear to be so far from her for the rest of our lives! And I do not want to leave Colorado. Well, we can only keep going and see how things work out for them. Perhaps Owen does not feel the same as she does and it will all come to nothing. Who's to know? Certainly not I.

Chapter Fifteen—Two Women in Love

Lois was uncharacteristically silent after they had departed the Anderton farm. Susan was a bit concerned about her. What was she thinking about? With the two of them it was usually no holds barred; not this time, apparently. Lois was keeping her thoughts to herself.

FOR PAINTING COW-SHED/ BARN OR FENCE/THAT SHAVING BRUSH/ IS JUST IMMENSE/ BURMA SHAVE.

Susan was having a fine time collecting new Burma Shave signs as they rode along. Other than that, the scenery did not offer much diversion until they went through a town. When they stopped for lunch at a small park in one of those little settlements (Susan forgot to record which one) to partake of some of the food Aunt Frances had plied them with, Lois finally expressed what was on her mind.

"Sue, I think I'm in love. Don't you think he's the most wonderful man you ever met?" Susan smiled enigmatically, for of course in her mind Ravi fit that description. "He's certainly a good man," she replied, "and nice-looking to boot. But isn't it a little too soon to be in love? After all, he didn't give any indication that he was attracted to you. And we only just met him." She grimaced at her hypocrisy, because in her mind she was already planning her wedding to Ravi, a detail she had not chosen to share with Lois. Now didn't seem to be the time. Plus, there were some issues to work out, such as where they would live, and whether his parents would accept her, a woman not of their faith. And whether Ravi was as taken with her as she was with him…

"Don't rain on my parade, please," Lois answered, a bit sharply for her. "I'm already planning our wedding. I'm going to start designing my dress as soon as we get home." Susan could see that there was no possibility of dissuading Lois, so she pulled out the trusty map to estimate how far to the next town. "Since we didn't have to pay for lodging last night, can we find a motel tonight?" she asked. Lois, munching on a luscious egg salad sandwich carefully packed in ice by Aunt Frances, nodded in a rather distracted way and put the food down. Teddy was the beneficiary of the rest of her sandwich. For dessert they had a few of the oatmeal cookies Aunt Frances had sent along with them. She made them with brown sugar, she had confided, when she could get it. They were soft and chewy and flavored just right.

Once in a while, the two friends gravitated into serious conversations. That had not happened so far on the road trip, but on Day Ten they were setting out their picnic when Susan said, "Do you think they'll ever fix it?"

Without asking, Lois understood what Susan referred to. "I don't know. It's such a mess. How can anyone find jobs for millions of men, or food for so many hungry people? What could help the banks stay open and feel safe for people? Where will everyone live?"

"Even if the drought ends soon, which it's surely got to, how can the farmers catch up and make a living again? Papa owed the bank for three years of seeds. I don't know why they hadn't taken the farm before he died."

"My guess is the bank just didn't know what to do with it. They probably foreclosed on lots of farms, and the land just sat there, blowing away. What use was it to them?"

"I see what you mean. It would just be one more deserted farm on the rolls, no way to sell it or farm it."

"Owen seems to have found a way to do it, though," Lois remarked. "He is a really smart farmer."

"One of the smartest, I think," Susan agreed, noting the way Lois's face softened and her eyes shone when she spoke about Owen Anderton. "There have to be better agricultural practices to beat the

131

drought. In Colorado and Kansas we've had the Mormon cricket and grasshoppers, on top of everything else. Maybe there's a way to keep them from eating everything in sight."

"I've read that land grant colleges like the one in Fort Collins are researching better ways to farm," Lois replied. "But I'm afraid it's going to take a few years for that to help. How will we all hang on until then?"

Susan shook her head. "Well, you and I can't save the world. All we can do is live the best we can and help if possible. That's not much, but if I've learned one thing on this trip it's that people are mostly good and they usually mean well even if they don't always show it. They help sometimes when they really don't have any help to spare. In Chicago I saw an older woman walking along the street putting her hand on lamp posts as she went along. Sometimes she would stop and rest for a few minutes and lean on one. I was just about to stop and ask she needed assistance when another older woman came along. She was bent over, almost toothless, and wearing a very ragged dress. She went over to the woman who was leaning against a post and asked if she could help. I was so touched and so amazed."

"What did the leaning woman say?"

"She shook her head and thanked the older woman. She put her hand on the woman's arm and told her that she had just had some bad news and would be all right after a while. Then she offered to buy the helping woman a cup of coffee and a donut, and they went off together." Tears glistened at the corners of Susan's eyes; she brushed at them impatiently. "That really moved me."

"Yes. I agree with you about people. That sheriff is the only really bad one we've met so far except for the guy who tried to get into our stash. He was just desperate, I think." She paused. "Not to say there aren't bad people, lots of them, like some of the profs we had in college. But the good ones definitely outnumber them. Maybe the bad ones even started out good, and things happened to them along the way to change their behavior. But people are resilient; this trip has shown me how tough we Americans can be. We just make the best of things and go from day to day."

"I've been wanting to talk about this but wasn't sure you were ready to hear it. You're always so sunny and cheerful."

"Not always, Sue. I've had times when I got pretty low. Growing up, having a mother like Gloria and a father who didn't give a fig about me, I could get really lonely and sad. But one day I just decided that feeling sorry for myself was boring and pointless so I wasn't going to do it any more. I decided to choose to be happy."

"That," declared Susan, "deserves a hug. I wish you knew how many times you have brought me out of the doldrums. I think I'm going to decide to be happy too, no matter what happens."

With that, they hugged (always a challenging experience: Lois had to bend down a long way to accomplish it), cleaned up from the picnic—having made sure that Teddy had been fed and had water to drink—and started down the road once more.

As luck would have it, rain started pouring down on them after they had gone another hundred miles or so. Camping was clearly out of the question, so they began looking for a suitable motel. When they saw a sign that said," Pets Welcome," Lois pulled in. The name of the motel was unimaginative—just "Route 66 Motel"—but it would do. This room had twin beds, to Susan's relief. The ubiquitous kitchenette allowed them to make a hot meal of canned beans and crackers with peanut butter, and Teddy settled down between the beds with a happy sigh.

"I think he likes us," Lois said.

"I think he loves us." Susan patted Teddy's fuzzy head, and he looked up at her with what could easily have passed for a doggy smile. When all were contentedly fed and tucked in, so to speak, they drifted off to the sound of rain on the roof. But by morning it had stopped raining, and the canvas covering on the back of the truck, though a bit soggy, had kept their supplies from getting soaked. Neither acknowledged it, but the trip was getting tiring. Two weeks turned out to be a long time on the road; both were ready to be home again. But they still had to get through Illinois and cross Missouri, Kansas and Eastern Colorado, so it would be several more days. Once again they were on the hunt for a place to wash their clothes; despite their preference for being indoors they decided that if the weather was clear they would camp because campgrounds generally had washtubs, whereas at a motel the only choice was a small sink, all right for undies but not for trousers or shirts.

The next time they stopped, for gas, Lois decided they should take pictures of each other in their travel gear. Though she remained cheerful, her shoulders drooped a bit and her eyes revealed her fatigue. Susan began to worry about her friend. When they found a picnic spot, she asked Lois if she wanted her to drive for a while. That perked Lois right up. "Oh, no. You're doing a fine job navigating; I'll be all right." Susan imagined her friend had a vision of her very short friend sitting in the driver's seat, barely able to reach the pedals or shift the gears, much less see over the wheel. True enough, but she had thought she should make the offer.

Along with photos, Lois had been collecting penny postcards. She planned to put them in an album when they got home again. It would be, along with the pictures, a perfect memento of their grand adventure. She picked up postcards wherever she could and put them in with the rest, scribbling a brief note on the back to note the date, place and time. Not by nature an organized person, Lois was meticulous about recording their journey via the pictures she took and the postcards she bought. Susan found that trait an intriguing aspect of her friend's personality.

It was almost completely dark by the time they found a campground, chose a spot, and pitched the tent, too late to start a fire and have a hot supper, leaving them to eat cold tinned corned beef and the last of the cookies. Teddy seemed not to mind, though.

They'd forgotten how uncomfortable it was to sleep on the bare ground. The air was hot and clammy; they both lay on top of their bedrolls in their clothes. For reasons neither could articulate, they were uneasy and slept lightly, Lois with the baseball bat beside her, Susan with one hand resting gently on Teddy's back. He had chosen to join them in the tent that night.

A shout and a scream, almost simultaneously, woke them. They sat bolt upright; Teddy took a protective stance between them. "What in the world is happening?" Susan whispered.

"Don't know. I'll peek out and see." Lois wiggled over to the tent door and peered out. What she saw sent her scurrying back in. "Everybody's out of the tents. There's a man with a gun telling them to give him their money or he'll shoot."

At that moment came another shout. "Get out here! Right now!"

Lois swallowed hard. "I think he means us." So the two friends made their way out of the tent, only to be faced with a menacing handgun pointed directly at them. "Gimme your money. Put it in that pile over there." He gestured to the left with his free hand. Lois had no intention whatsoever of surrendering what funds they had left. She shook her head. "We have no money."

"Like hell! Everyone's got money. Fork it over, sister." He waved the gun around in the air.

That was enough for Teddy. Pulling the leash loose from Susan's hand, he headed straight for the gunman's legs. "Oh, god, he'll shoot him," moaned Susan, her hand at her throat.

Not if Teddy had anything to do with it. He fastened his teeth firmly onto the man's left ankle and bit down, hard. "Yow!" came a yell. Teddy hung on fast. The gun fell from the man's hand, which was encouragement enough for two young men who'd been standing together in front of their tent to come forward and tackle the miscreant, forcing him to the ground. Teddy let go, satisfied. The larger man planted himself on the robber's back and sat. More curses issued forth from underneath him. The other young man picked up the gun and threw it as far as he could. The rest of the campers, about a dozen in all, hurried to retrieve their money, then went back inside their tents. The two men looked at each other. "What should we do with him?"

Lois had an idea. "Take off his shoes and send him on down the road," she suggested. "Make sure he can't find that gun anywhere, though, or he might come back here or rob someone else." She had a moment's qualms, thinking that perhaps they should have notified the authorities about the incident, but their last encounter with a county sheriff had not gone well, so she decided against it.

"What do you think, Butch?" said the upright man to his companion. "Sounds good to me," was the reply. Accordingly, he removed the robber's shoes, leaving him with feet covered only by holey stockings, and stood him up. "Get out of here," he told the robber. "Get on down the road."

Limping, snarling and cursing, the robber walked away. Butch, who had been holding him down, rose and extended a hand to Lois." Isaac Moore," he said. "Butch and I are on our way to Hollywood. Hoping to get into films, don'cha know." (Privately, Susan thought he would never make it, because he had a very nasal, rather high-pitched voice which would not work well since the advent of talking pictures.) Butch headed into the foliage where he had thrown the firearm to secrete it safely and was gone for a time, returning eventually with the pistol. "Let him try to rob someone with this," he declared. "Threw away the bullets," he said. "We'll take it along with us. Might be a good prop."

"Was the gun really loaded?" Lois asked him. He nodded. "Yeah, it was. Three bullets in it. He probably knew how to use it too," he added. "My real name's Jason Lawrence. Ike just calls me Butch—sounds more Hollywood, he says," he told Susan and Lois, who in turn introduced themselves. Isaac knelt down to pat Teddy. "Some dog you got there." "He sure is," Susan said. "This is the second time he's saved us."

Lois turned to her friend. "What time is it? I don't think I can get back to sleep now; we might as well pack up and get on the road." Susan informed her that it was 4:40 a.m.; the sun would be up soon. Together they began collecting their gear and taking down the tent. "Don't forget we need to do laundry," Susan reminded her. "That's why we camped last night." Susan commented, while they washed out their clothes, that she didn't think the aspiring movie stars would get very far in their quest. They were both nice-looking, sure, but they were young, naïve and inexperienced. "They'd have to get really, really lucky," Lois agreed. "I'm not much impressed with them; they just stood there and let that man hold a gun on them.

They didn't even try to resist." Susan nodded. "That's true. Nobody did, until we came out with Teddy."

After a light breakfast of tinned fruit and bread with peanut butter and jelly, they once again set out with laundry waving merrily behind them. Once again, they enjoyed a hearty laugh about the sight. It was a relief to laugh after the tension during the night, which they didn't talk about the rest of the day. That adventure had come too close to disaster for comfort.

We've talked about how most people are good, or at least they want to be, and what nice ones we've met on this trip. But we met another bad one last night. Maybe he was really hungry, maybe he was desperate, but he didn't have to threaten us with a gun. We would have helped him if he'd just asked. I confess to being frightened from tip to toe. No doubt L was too, but she's better at concealing it than I am. Thank goodness for dear Teddy.

So much we didn't expect has happened on this trip! Who would believe it? If someone made a movie or wrote a book about all these encounters on one road trip, it would never see the light of day. Helping a woman give birth, finding a splendid dog, being as good as accused of murder, almost getting robbed, both of us meeting the men we want to marry…Whew! When we tell our friends after we get home, they will just laugh at us and think we made it all up.

Chapter Sixteen—No More Camping Out

Laundry, they agreed, could wait until they were home again. For the rest of the trip they would choose motels, even if they had to clean rooms to pay for them.

THE CANNONEERS/ WITH WIRY BEARDS AND HAIRY EARS/ ON WIRE WHISKERS/ USED TIN SHEARS/ UNTIL THEY FOUND/ BURMA SHAVE.

Susan noted that Lois's hands were shaking a little as she gripped the steering wheel. "Feels like we're in a moving picture," she remarked after a while. "Who would imagine all these things that keep happening to us? Who would make a film with such a ridiculous plot? No one would believe it." She chuckled.

"Well," Lois replied, "I hope we have come to the end and will have no more excitement. That last scene was almost more than I could take. It felt like I was in a dream." Susan "hmmed" and nodded her agreement, then turned again to scroll the scenery as they went by. Water towers with names on them identified towns; silos rose on farmland. Here and there cattle grazed, and they saw a mother duck leading her ducklings lazily to a pond. Suddenly Lois pulled off to the side of the road. She snatched the camera, hastily got out of the truck, and headed toward a nearby pasture. "Did you ever see anything so magnificent?" she breathed, aiming her camera skyward. And indeed what came into their vision was breathtaking—a whole flock of swans had taken to the air and were flying in formation. They formed a perfect "V" as they flew. "Like geese at home,"

Susan said. Behind the flying birds was the most perfect rainbow either of them had ever seen. Lois snapped shot after shot. "Maybe I can color that when we get home.

"Well, that almost makes up for last night," she commented as she got back in the driver's seat.

They spent the night in another nondescript overnight stop, this one called The Rodeside Inn. ("Deliberately misspelled?" grumbled Susan. "As if it were the only one," Lois commented wryly.) It was cheap, only $1 a night, but they soon saw why: the mattress was lumpy, the towels were see-through thin, hot water was nonexistent, only one burner worked on the stove, the curtains wouldn't close all the way, and the linoleum was cracked. "Not our best stop," Lois said as they departed in the morning. "At least we were indoors, with a door that locked. Less chance of being robbed again," Susan replied. "That place goes in the books as our worst motel so far."

"I can't imagine any that would be much worse than that one." Lois sighed; then she smiled her world-class best. "We'll laugh about it when we get home again."

"We can laugh about it now. I'd rather laugh than think about that gun. I kept dreaming about it last night. All I could see was that thing pointed straight at me."

"You were tossing and turning a lot. I wondered if you were having a bad dream. I should have waked you up."

"I'm sorry I bothered you. No need for your sleep to be disturbed too. You were the brave one, refusing to give him your money."

"The bravest one was our Teddy. He's the best dog in the world." Lois briefly rubbed Teddy's curly head, not taking her eyes off the road. Susan gave him an affectionate hug, earning in return a slobbery kiss. "You are the best part of this whole trip," she informed him. He wagged his tail. Privately, she amended her statement to include meeting Ravi, but she didn't voice that thought.

LAWYERS, DOCTORS/ SHEIKS AND BAKERS/MOUNTAINEERS AND UNDERTAKERS/MAKE THEIR BRISTLY BEARDS BEHAVE/BY USING BRUSHLESS/ BURMA SHAVE.

They knew that once they left Route 66 they would see no more Burma Shave signs; Susan was delightedly noting them all in her journal, and sometimes Lois stopped to take a snapshot of one. They certainly provided entertainment and amusement along the way.

That day was, to their relief, entirely uneventful. Theda ticked along obligingly (although Owen had given them a wrench to use and shown Lois how to use it, just in case); they encountered very little traffic, and the heat was relieved somewhat by a light, intermittent cool breeze. When they reached Joplin they said farewell to the famous highway and headed west on considerably poorly maintained roads. No matter—the roads were taking them home. They could endure ruts, and narrow lanes, and occasional holes (which Lois had become expert at evading), as long as they knew each mile was taking them closer to their destination. Missouri was hot and sticky. They crossed it in two long, scorching days, spending the night at a boarding house in a small town in yet another nondescript, unmemorable small town, this one drooping with discouragement and discontent. While civil enough, the few people they came across were not friendly or hospitable. The proprietor of the boarding house, a middle-aged woman who looked to Susan for all the world like the witch who lured Hansel and Gretel into her house, spoke in monotones, provided a meager breakfast at best—toast with butter, some tired-looking apple slices, and weak coffee—, and never once cracked even a minimal smile. When they crossed the border into Kansas, they both sighed with relief, though they were not entirely sure why.

Kansas was visibly drier than when they had passed through several days earlier. Corn stalks drooped even more, and wheat listed to one side or the other. No breeze came along to relieve the heat. After a quick picnic under a small shade tree, they came at last to the Crandall General Store. Susan found her heart rate quicken and her palms sweaty as the store came closer, and her heart fell to her boots when she saw that the family sedan was not parked around on the side of the building, although several cars were parked here and there nearby. "Maybe it's just his father who's gone," she said hopefully. Lois nodded her encouragement. She had known all along that Susan was smitten with Ravi; she'd just been waiting for Susan to bring it up.

Inside, people of various sizes and ages milled around while Pariz Crandall collected their purchases, one customer at a time. Large men dressed in coveralls and open-collared shirts, women in what could only be flour-sack dresses, loose and unbelted; girls with dresses similar to their mothers', boys in knee pants and suspenders over colorful buttoned shirts stood in small clumps, chatting and gesturing. The men were grouped together around the stone-cold pot-bellied stove in the center of the store, several puffing away on pipes. The women stood in smaller clumps, two or three together here and there, one eye on their offspring, the other on their companions. Meanwhile the children mostly stood longingly in front of the glass counter, behind which assorted penny candies were displayed. They probably hoped that if they behaved themselves, they might get a piece of candy and appeared to be busily deciding which kind they wanted.

While she was carrying a customer's purchases to the cash register Pariz turned her head and saw Lois and Susan. With a glad cry she set down the merchandise and ran over to give each of them a warm hug. "You came back! Oh, I am so delighted to see you!" Then she paused. "But Ravi and my husband have gone to get supplies. They won't be back until tomorrow. I am so sorry you have missed them."

"As am I," said Susan under her breath. Her disappointment could hardly have been more profound. She nudged Lois. "We really can't stay this time. We're on our way home and have to be there by Sunday so we can go back to work on Monday."

"I understand," Pariz replied. "I will give Ravi your greetings." With a gracious gesture of farewell, she turned back to her customers. "My apologies for keeping you waiting," she told the family whose merchandise she had just collected.

Clearly, it was time for the travelers to depart.

They spent that night at a farmhouse on the edge of a small Kansas town which had a sign in front that offered overnight accommodations, along with breakfast, for $1.50. "Don't hold with dogs in the house," the woman informed them. They turned to go; if Teddy was not welcome, they would not stay. The woman cleared her throat and said, "Guess it'll be all right this time, though." They turned back into the house, concluding that she needed the money more than she needed to keep one small dog out of her home.

It was a quiet night, the prairie sounds lulling them to sleep. Lois found she was finally becoming accustomed to the noises of crickets, night birds and four-legged wild creatures. This house, along the side of the road, had an addition to the chorus from a herd of milk cows, who periodically called to each other in deep-voiced moos (at least, Lois supposed that's what they were doing). Still, she was able to get a good night's sleep and enjoy a savory breakfast of biscuits with gravy, fat sausages and scrambled eggs, along with memorable coffee, for which the farmer's wife even had rich cream, a real treat. Mostly, Susan and Lois drank their coffee black for lack of cream and sugar, but this time they indulged and were richly rewarded by the flavors.

The farmer's wife, who introduced herself as Delores (no last name offered), looked worn down and weary. She had pulled her stringy gray hair back into a bun, wore no makeup and had on a loose print dress underneath a voluminous butcher's apron. They saw no evidence of a husband until, when they had finished their meal, Delores fixed a tray of food and headed toward the back of the house. Innate curiosity getting the better of her, Susan peered around the corner and saw the woman enter a bedroom with the tray. "Must be her husband," she whispered. "Wonder what happened to him. Would it be too rude to ask?"

"Yes," Lois answered, "but let's do it anyway. Maybe we can help."

Delores returned to the kitchen, her face a grim mask. They decided not to ask; it seemed intrusive. Lois handed her hostess two one-dollar bills. "Just a little extra, for feeding two of us," she said. "Thank you for a great breakfast. And for letting us keep Teddy with us." She longed to ask whether Delores had help with the cows, or the crops, and how long her husband had been laid up, what was wrong with him, but she held her tongue. Delores pocketed the money in her apron and almost managed a small smile but said nothing.

As they were getting into the truck, a beaten-up truck of a different vintage and make than theirs pulled into the driveway, and a cadaverously thin, unusually tall man got out, followed by a large yellow dog, which promptly headed toward the barn.

"Boarding here, were you?" he called to them. Lois nodded. "Did Ma feed you good?" Lois nodded again. "Glad to hear it," the man said, and he strode into the house. They felt better to know that Delores had some help. Whatever had gone wrong with her husband, there was someone around to help with the farm work. Grim though the woman was, her room had been comfortable enough, and the food was delicious and hearty. So it was a relief to see that she was not alone with her burden. Tender-hearted Susan especially disliked seeing people in distress and always wanted to make things better if she could. Even though her sunny view of human nature had faltered a bit on the road trip, she still believed that the majority of people were well-meaning, if not always considerate, generous or kind.

The hours passed smoothly enough, with occasional conversation and a picnic at lunch followed by the discovery of a restroom and gas station, despite the uneven roads and the unrelenting heat.

"I can't say I would ever be able to live with this heat," Lois commented during their picnic stop, "but it doesn't feel quite as bad as it did at first. I must be getting a little bit used to it."

They both openly cheered when they crossed the border into Colorado. The landscape was unchanged, dry, windblown, brown, but they were on their way home at last, and it was wonderful to be back. When a somewhat seedy motel appeared on the horizon they decided to pass the night there rather than keep looking as it got darker. Although looking rundown, the exterior badly in need of paint, their room was sparkling clean, everything worked (even hot water for the shower) and it was quiet and peaceful in that squat building out on the endless prairie. Susan had gotten used to hanging onto the edge of the bed when she shared it with Lois; this room, though, had two decorous twin beds, so she once again luxuriated in having enough room overnight. The motel, the name of which they never learned (the sign simply said "Motor Hotel") did not provide breakfast, so they found a nearby café which did and ordered sparingly, since Lois said their funds were dwindling rapidly. They shared a plate of pancakes, served with sausage, but each enjoyed a fresh cup of coffee—with cream and sugar. Lois was able to secrete a good-sized sausage in her pocket (wrapped in a napkin, which they vowed they would wash and return) for Teddy, who appeared to greatly enjoy the treat. Lois carefully noted the town and name of the café so they could send back the napkin (which they did), and they rolled on westward.

Ravi was gone when we got there! I was so longing to see him. My heart cracked. I will write him a letter—no, maybe just a postcard—and let him know I am thinking of him. Which I do, a great deal. Oh, it will be so good to get home again. What will we do about Teddy, though? We're not supposed to have pets. Oh, dear, what shall we do? He will stay with us even if we have to move. He saved our lives; we could never let him go to anyone else.

Road Trip

Chapter Seventeen—Home Again

They pushed hard to get home, choosing not to stop even as dusk descended. They had to get home, so they had to keep going. As they approached Denver, the familiar jagged skyline came into view. Almost simultaneously, they breathed a sigh of joy and relief. To see the mountains after going through so much flat country was reassuring to say the least. Colorado had never looked so good. Neither traveler regretted the trip, not at all, but they relished the heady joy of coming home to the familiar, the reliable and the comfortable.

Susan's thoughts turned to her own small bedroom and her cozy single bed, with the quilt her mother had made her before arthritis rendered her almost immobile, unable to use her nimble fingers any longer. She'd often thought that if she had become a doctor she would have searched for a cure for that dreadful disease, but, like Lois, she'd been persuaded away from such an ambition by the thought of all the blood and gore it would entail. Besides which, her gender worked against her. Women simply did not become doctors unless they were extraordinarily talented and tenacious. Of course she had seen plenty of unpleasant sights on the farm—that was part of being a farmer—but she had always kept her distance from the necessary butchering. Enrico did it; before that, Papa. She knew, though, that they did it as quickly and humanely as possible.

Lois thought about sneaking Teddy in and how they could conceal him from the landlord, who did come around from time to time to check on his tenants.

It was fully dark by the time Lois pulled up in front of their building, which had six units, two on each floor. The front units faced Downing Street, while the back ones looked onto a small courtyard, beyond which was an intimate, tidy neighborhood park. Theirs was the third-floor unit in the back, which Lois regarded as quite the best of the apartments. They worked out a plan: The fire escape was in back of their apartment. Susan could go through the front door of the building into their apartment and let Lois in through the fire-escape door. That should work. Lois parked the Ford on the street in front of the yellow brick building and hopped out, gesturing at Susan to go in first and pointing toward Teddy and the back door. Susan nodded and went into the front lobby area, where two plants were withering (she had been the one to water them, and she had hoped Miss T. Young might have done it in her place, but apparently not) and the steep, narrow carpeted stairway led up to their apartment. The telephone sat quietly on the wall above the table where the mailman always set the day's mail for all the tenants, leaving them to sort it out. But she had no sooner stepped inside than Miss T. Young poked her head out from the apartment below theirs.

"You young ladies are home again, I see. Safe travels, I hope?" Susan nodded. "Where is Miss Parker? I have a message for her."

"She'll be along in a minute. She's organizing our gear so we can bring it all in." Miss T. Young held out a stack of envelopes. "I have your mail as well." Susan thanked her. "I'll tell Lois." She hurried up the stairs just in time to open the back door and let Lois and Teddy in.

Lois went downstairs and knocked on Miss T. Young's door. "You have a message for me?"

"You are to call your father as soon as you get home," she replied. "He said it was very important that you call him."

"When did he call?"

"Four days ago, Wednesday it was."

"Thank you, Miss Young. I appreciate it. I'll call him as soon as we get unloaded." Lois was a little taken aback—when had her remote, detached father ever called her since she left home? Not unduly concerned nonetheless, she bent to the task of unloading the truck and sorting out their belongings and supplies once they were all deposited in the apartment. Despite having two bedrooms, it was a small place, with an open kitchen barely big enough for a table and two chairs, a small living area dominated by the console radio, and a bathroom between the two small bedrooms. Sorting everything out took a while; they were both quite tired by the time order had been restored. Teddy was sitting by the door. "Oh, I guess he needs to go out," Susan said.

"I'll take him; you call your father."

It was Sunday night, rather late; Lois supposed her father would be at home but on the other hand, he might be at the office. He tended not to stay home much even on weekends. Still, she gave the operator that number first. The phone rang for several minutes with no answer. The number at the office yielded the same result. She had her foot on the first step of the stairway when the telephone rang; she answered it. The deep voice at the other end was her father's.

"Lois?"

"Yes, Father. I just tried calling you."

"I heard the telephone ring, but I was upstairs and did not get to it before the ringing stopped. I'd like you to come home."

"Why? What's happened?" Fear curled around Lois's heart.

"Your mother died four days ago of alcohol poisoning." She heard the distaste in his voice. "The funeral is next Saturday at the mortuary. She left you something in her will and I would like to give it to you."

Lois took in a deep breath. Poor Gloria, dead. "Are George or Stanley coming home for the funeral?"

"George is able to attend. It will take him two days on the train." Her father's voice was, as usual, dry and emotionless. He delivered the news about his wife's death and his son's plans as if he were talking about the weather. No surprise there, Lois thought, and no point in pursuing the subject. Long ago she had learned that she would never win where her father was concerned; he was like a dog with a bone, carrying his righteousness around with him almost triumphantly, never ceasing to harangue until the other party conceded the point due to complete exhaustion, so it was best to say nothing at all. She wasn't at all sure why George was coming, and she had no intention of asking. He had left home as soon as he could and not returned. If he loved his mother, Lois never discerned that. George was, like her father, unable or unwilling to express his feelings. As far as she knew, he lived for money and success, for recognition and approbation.

"Can you come to the house at 5 o'clock tomorrow to get what your mother left you? As for the funeral next Saturday, you should also come here. It would be best for the three of us to arrive at the funeral together." It would look best, Lois thought. "What about Susan? I want her there with me."

"Your mousy little librarian friend? I don't mind if she attends, but she can get there on her own."

But this time Lois was not prepared to give in, especially after the insult her father had just delivered. "If she doesn't come with me, I am not coming." A long, aggravated sigh came through the telephone line. "Oh, very well. Bring her along. Just be sure she is suitably dressed." Ever conscious of appearances, her father. But the reason didn't matter; he was permitting Susan to be with her. She wasn't sure she could get through it without her closest friend.

"Shouldn't I be feeling sad?" she asked Susan after she came back upstairs. "You felt sad when your mother died, didn't you?"

"My mother wasn't like yours. She was kind and good, and she loved us both. She often told us so. I cried when she died; of course I did, but I was almost out of tears because I had cried so much for Richard. Her death felt like one more blow. It almost drained me of sadness for a long time. My goal was to help Papa. If Enrico hadn't come along when he did, I would never have left the farm. Papa needed me." She paused, then took a deep, shuddering breath. "I don't think a person ever gets over losing someone she loved. The sadness is always there. But I learned to live with it and keep going. Mama wouldn't have wanted me to keep on being sad."

Tears were streaming down her cheeks as she spoke. Lois reached over and hugged her. "I feel as if I should be sad, or at least feel something, but Gloria was never really a mother to me, and she drank herself to death because she wouldn't even try to stop." Her tone was bitter. "I suppose she was better with George and Stanley, but by the time I came along she was drunk every day by noon. My father hired a nanny, and she fed me and changed me, so I got attached to her, but then she left and another one came, and another and another until I was old enough to go to school. Then he hired a cook and housekeeper. She was the one who saved me. Her name was Nora, and she was the mother I never had. She got me ready for school and walked me there, and when I came home after school she gave me cookies and milk and asked me about my day. Without her, I think I would have been a horrible child. But when I was thirteen Father sent me away to boarding school. He fired Nora and hired a cook and housekeeper who didn't live with us and a nurse for Mother.

"Every so often, Mother would get sober for a few days and play at motherhood, but she wasn't very good at it. Her way of mothering was to tell me how homely I was, how I would never get a husband because I'm so tall, and how being smart isn't a good way to get a man anyway. She seemed obsessed that I find a husband, yet all the time she told me I never would. Once in a while, she did do something nice for me; we went clothes shopping at May D&F one day and she bought me an elegant dress. I still have it, even though I don't wear it because the color doesn't suit me at all. She was even sober that day. One or two other times she had a spell of being motherly, but it never lasted very long. I never for a moment believed she loved me. I'm not sure she was capable of loving anyone, even herself."

"How did you turn out to be such a wonderful person?" Susan asked, her eyes wide with love and admiration.

"I'm hardly a wonderful person, but I decided not to let her drag me down. I wouldn't ruin my life the way she ruined hers, and if I ever got married, I would be a loving wife and the best mother anyone could be. My children will know every day that I love them."

"You told me once before that you'd decided to be happy," Susan replied, "but you never told me why. I don't think you need to feel the least bit guilty about not being sad that your mother is dead. At least she is at peace. A person has to be really miserable to take to the bottle like that, I think, so it might be a good thing that she isn't miserable any longer. We'll go to the funeral, wear black and say the right things, and then we'll just go on about our business."

"You always know the right thing to say, Sue. Thank you." Lois smiled slightly.

When they arrived at Lois's childhood home, a large, imposing stone house in Park Hill ("the right part of town") a flood of memories, most of them unpleasant, swamped Lois. Her father greeted her at the door. "Did you come in that—that thing out there?" Lois smiled. "We drove it all the way to Chicago and back. It got us where we wanted to go. She's a fine piece of machinery."

"Well, we'll go to the funeral in the limousine." Although her father had met Susan, Lois made a point of introducing them. Her father nodded at Susan but did not offer to shake her hand.

He gestured for them to come in. In the ornate living room that was as large as their whole apartment, he bade them sit down and took a box from the mantel piece. "This is what Gloria left you," he said. "I have no idea what's in it." Lois set it aside; she would not give her father the satisfaction of opening the box in front of him. A petty act, she knew, but she did it anyway. It was a small container, about the size of a box of cigars, made of metal. There was no lock on the clasp, no rattling when she picked it up. She set it on the side table next to her, thanked her father for giving it to her, and stood to leave. "I'll see you at the funeral," she told him. The service was to be at one of the largest Presbyterian churches in town. Gloria had not been a practicing anything, but Lois's father attended the church ostentatiously from time to time, for business and political reasons, and he prevailed on the pastor to conduct a service for his wife. Lois had no idea what possessed her father to choose such a vast place for his wife's funeral when she was certain only a handful of people would come.

Road Trip

Meantime, the two adventurers had to get back to their everyday lives. While The Boss did not welcome Susan back or grace her with anything resembling a smile, he did comment that work had piled up while she was gone and she'd better get busy catching up. Susan breathed a sigh of relief; she had not admitted to Lois how worried she was that her job—which she needed despite its being so low-paying, with a difficult boss to put it kindly—would not be waiting for her when they returned. But it was. After all, Lois commented later, "Who else could he get to work there in such conditions?" (Which did not, actually, comfort Susan much...)

As for Lois, her department head grudgingly welcomed her back with a comment that sales had been down noticeably while she was away. "Time for you to turn on your charm," she told Lois with a grimace that obviated the compliment. Customers had come in, the other women on the floor told her, but they weren't buying. Some had even asked for Miss Parker. Lois, who had not admitted to Susan that she too had been rather apprehensive about her job not being there when she got back home, said a silent "thank you" to the atmosphere. It wasn't the greatest job in the world, but it was a job for which she was grateful in these hard times. It helped pay the rent and put food on the table. A job was a job in 1932. For a moment, Helen Perry flashed through her mind. She wondered whether the woman had found a job yet. She hoped so. Lois was grateful for her job, even if it was selling the latest fashions to fussy, narcissistic women in a department store.

Turnout for the funeral was small as Lois had suspected, mostly her father's work associates and their wives. Some people from the country club, where Gloria had gone to play golf during her brief spells of sobriety, were there, too. The sparse crowd looked lost in the enormous, ornately decorated church sanctuary. Regardless of the heat—for it was now July and stiflingly warm even though to the two travelers it felt much more tolerable than Midwestern heat—the women wore long-sleeved, somber black dresses, gloves, and suitably decorous hats; the men were attired in business suits, tie, vest, jacket and all. (Lois did notice a bow tie here and there.) Lois and Susan had donned simple black sheath dresses purchased by Lois at the department store for a significant discount, for such attire had not been selling well for some time.

An elaborate spray of flowers sat on top of the casket, which was brought in and carried out again by four hefty young men who sat in the back of the room in silence, even during the obligatory hymns and readings. In an aside to Susan, Lois commented that her father had no doubt hired them to be pall bearers. The service meant nothing to Lois. Gloria had not been religious, and the words the minister spoke about eternal life did not reflect whatever she had believed, if anything at all. George, Lois's brother, was tall and domineering like his father, with a hearty handshake, a fake smile and a suitably mournful tone when he spoke of his mother. He sported a dark, thin, Clark-Gable mustache.

George made no overture to his sister. He greeted her merely with, "Hello, Lois. How are you?" then turned away before she could answer. Though they sat next to each other during the service (Susan on Lois's other side), George said not a word. He did not offer to give a eulogy and Lois saw no signs of sorrow in his expression. Once again she wondered why on earth he had come.

The funeral cortege went to the cemetery for the burial; Lois noticed that her father had ordered a large headstone with floral carvings. After the brief graveside ritual, the bereaved husband had arranged for a reception at his home, with coffee, tea and cookies, but Lois chose not to attend. She had nothing to say to her brother, who had not contacted her once since he went to California, and she had said all she was going to say to her father. She left him, standing tall and smiling, glad-handing his work colleagues, introducing his son, and accepting condolences with hypocritical ease—false condolences Lois could not have borne to listen to. They were meaningless social patter; those people never knew her mother, not really, and if they had, they probably would not have liked her much. The minister had spoken generously of her lively spirit, philanthropic works and love of beauty, attributes Lois had never seen. What was there to say? So she and Susan left in the limousine, where the driver had been waiting in a shady spot. He rather begrudgingly took them home to their apartment.

When they got back home, Lois opened the box her father had handed her. Inside, she found several pieces of exquisite, expensive jewelry—a pearl necklace, diamond earrings, several rings with varied gem stones, a turquoise necklace, and a gold filigreed brooch shaped like an aspen leaf, all nestled in a bed of ivory-colored satin. Lois's eyes widened in amazement; she had never seen Gloria wear any of that jewelry. On the rare occasions when she and her father went out together, Gloria wore costume jewelry—dangling earrings made of silver, a lapel pin made of fake pearls (Lois knew they were fake because Gloria had told her so), or a black satin choker which had one gem in the center; Lois thought it was a garnet. Lois was stunned by the bequest; the jewelry was worth a great deal of money. She carefully replaced everything and closed up the box, setting it on the kitchen counter while she decided what to do with it. She turned her attention to what Susan was saying, something about Teddy.

Going to work, they'd left Teddy at home hoping he would stay quiet. He must have, for no one had complained when they got home again. But this time he seemed extra glad to see them. Lois tucked him under her shirt and slipped out the back door to take him to the park, where he could do his business and know the joy of being outdoors. They would just have to hope for the best until they could find another place, one where he would be allowed. Working all day meant leaving him at home, which meant he might bark while they were gone, but as far as they knew Miss T. Young and the other tenants were gone all day too, so maybe it would be all right.

However, a few weeks after they'd both started back to work a man came out of the front first-floor apartment and stepped in front of them as they came down the stairs to go to work. "Did I hear a dog up there?"

Lois tried to look innocent. "A dog?"

"Yeah. A dog. Barking."

"Well…"

"Thought so. Tell you what, though—if you won't turn me in for having two cats, I won't turn you in for having a dog."

"He's a really little dog," Susan said, "and he saved us from a robber with a gun."

"Besides," added Lois, "he is extremely well behaved."

"Sure. I wouldn't have heard him if I hadn't been home sick for two days. Head cold." At that point, he issued forth a mighty sneeze. Lois and Susan backed up even though he had turned his head away from them. "Sorry," he said and stepped back inside his apartment, shutting the door.

Now they knew they had to find another apartment, and soon. Lois began scanning the newspaper that very evening. The search occupied their time for several days, until they came upon a garden-level place with two bedrooms that allowed pets (small ones only) for the same rent they were paying. It was in Capitol Hill, on a quiet side street. "Perfect," they agreed. They gave notice and were moved within a month (with considerable help from several of Lois's hefty male friends). Now Teddy could look out the glass doors while they were gone and go for a romp the minute they got home again.

Their new apartment looked out onto a small back yard which was profuse with hardy flowers in spite of the drought. Their new kitchen was a real treat, with a large counter, double sink, full-sized refrigerator and four-burner gas stove. Plenty of cupboard space, too. The living room was big enough for Lois's console radio to fit without taking up most of the space, as it had in the other place, and their dining table nestled nicely against a kitchen wall. All in all a sweet deal, Lois said.

Susan noticed that Lois seemed somewhat distracted, sometimes even moody, and concluded that her friend was grieving, whether she knew it or not. Losing a parent, as Susan well knew, left a person bereft, alone and feeling orphaned, a small skiff adrift on an enormous, roiling sea without anyone coming to the rescue, no harbor in sight and no anchor available even had there been a harbor. Lois might as well be an orphan, given the father she had. But Lois was grieving not for Gloria but for the life she had never had, love she had never known, hope for a mother's nurturing care finally, irrevocably gone. Susan knew, though, that Lois would soon get beyond her sorrow. Grief never leaves, but the bereaved learn to live with it, as she knew so well.

And soon enough, Lois's choice to be happy rose to the fore. She became again her sunny self, reported unusual success at the department store, told lively stories about her customers, and bustled around making their new apartment cozy and homey, a domestic side of her that Susan had not seen before.

One day, Lois came home from work and told Susan, "I have something to tell you." Susan, who had been close to revealing her feelings for Ravi for days, sat down at the table and got a glass of water.

"What is it?" she said, although she was almost certain she knew.

"I can't stand it any more. I can't stop thinking about Owen. I want to write to him. Do you think I should do that?" Susan threw back her head with a joyous laugh. "I've been thinking the same thing about Ravi," she said when she had caught her breath. "By all means, we should write. Why did we wait so long?"

Lois made a face. "I guess I was afraid to find out if it was real, or just a fantasy I had when we were traveling."

Susan replied, "That's just how I felt. What if I imagined the whole thing? Tingling in the air—how silly is that? But I keep thinking about him and hoping it was real. We took a chance on having an adventure; why can't we take a chance on love?" She paused for a moment, then added, "I have the very thing. You collected all those penny postcards on the trip, why don't we each send one? If we don't get an answer, we'll know it was all just a passing fancy"— although in her heart of hearts Susan could not accept that it had been all a lovely dream. Lois nodded eagerly. She looked through the stack of postcards and selected one that featured the Navy Pier on Lake Michigan, her favorite sight on their trip. She addressed the card to the Anderton Farm in Hillsdale, Illinois: Attention Owen

155

Anderton, and wrote, in her precise, flowery hand, "Safely home, moved to a new place okay for Teddy. Back to work. Thanks to you & Aunt Frances for your hospitality," followed by their new address. She might have written down their former address when they stayed there; she wasn't sure, but they had moved, and that gave her a good excuse to write.

As for Susan, she picked a sepia card of a Kansas wheat field that she had bought at the Crandall store and wrote, "We were chugging along/Going our way /When we heard the crickets singing/They seemed to say..." She signed it "Susan Mayfield" and ended with their new address and mailed the postcard before losing her nerve. Never had she done such a bold thing before. Never.

Ravi might have been just a lovely dream, a foolish school-girl notion. Why would I suppose he would leave his parents to marry me? They depend on him to run the store, and they are Muslims, very religious. I'm not. I certainly couldn't live there, with no library anywhere near. We hardly saw any libraries in the small towns we drove through, although I did see a bookmobile on the road once or twice. What a wonderful idea that was, to bring books to children who would never get to read them otherwise! Well, I can only wait and hope. But whatever happens, I will not ever forget that singing in my heart when I first saw him. He is my first love. Perhaps—dare I hope—my only love. How do I know? I just do.

As for L, I think she feels the same way I do, anxious but hopeful. How crazy it would be if both of us found our future husbands on that fairy-tale trip!

Road Trip

Chapter Eighteen—The Rest of the Story

In the mail soon after they had sent the postcards came a package for Lois which contained a small framed needlework piece, no doubt done by Aunt Frances, of the farmhouse, along with a note for Lois that encouraged her, to say the least: "I'm glad your Ford got you home safely. Fondly, Owen."

To say Lois was excited would be to seriously understate the case. She jumped up and down, hugged Susan, hugged Teddy, and twirled around in circles. "How should I answer this?" she worried." I don't want to come across as forward, but I do want to let him know I am interested." They pondered her reply for days, finally coming up with a response that satisfied both of them. They decided a real letter was in order even if a stamp did cost three cents.

"Dear Aunt Frances and Owen," she began, "what a delight it was to receive the needlework of the farmhouse where we enjoyed such a happy interlude. We are sorting through the pictures I took to put them in an album so we will long remember our road trip. I will send you some.

"Teddy bit a man who was trying to rob us one night when we were camping, and he warns us when strangers are around. When we got home, we found a different apartment where we could keep him; he is with us for as long as he lives. He is a happy dog now, living with us.

"Both of us still had jobs when we got home, thank goodness, and we have been kept quite busy. We really like our new apartment and so does Teddy. Perhaps you can come visit us sometime.

"I hope you both are well and prospering on the farm even though things still look bleak in the nation. Money is tight, but we are getting along all right."

She signed it, "Sincerely, Lois Parker."

Only a week or so later, a letter came from Owen in which he expressed his happiness at getting a prompt reply from her. "We have always had dogs," he wrote. "Most farmers don't have them in the house, but ours live with us. Aunt Frances loves dogs, and they seem to love her. When you were at our farm, our German Shepherd, Rover, was in the barn tending to her puppies. We are trying to find good homes for them." Once again he signed the letter, "Fondly, Owen." He didn't comment on her invitation to come to Denver.

Meanwhile, Susan haunted the mailbox looking for a reply to the daring postcard she had sent to Ravi. Days went by with no response. Her belief in the magic that had happened between them began to flag. She was delighted, thrilled, for her friend, but heartsick when she looked, day after day, for mail that did not come.

Until, one day, it did. Ravi had sent back a postcard from the store. It said only, "You have stolen my heart/Don't go astray /As we sing love's old sweet song/Along the way." Susan was ecstatic. Without consulting Lois first she wrote back right away on another penny postcard. "I was so hoping you feel as I do," she began. She wrote of her eagerness to hear from him, her anxiety when nothing came, and her hopes for a future together.

He replied a few days later, in a sealed letter, that it had taken him so long to answer her postcard because he knew it meant leaving his parents and their store for a new life. He wanted, he told her, to become a doctor; he had wanted that from the time he was in secondary school. He would like to come live with her in the city—after marrying her, of course. Susan chuckled at the thought of Ravi becoming a doctor, a career she had long ago set aside. Ravi would be a perfect doctor.

In the dark of night Susan had given it a good deal of thought; she was certain that she could never live in tiny Hallelujah! Kansas, which did not even have a library, and give her life over to helping run a grocery store in a remote little town so far from civilization.

Nor could she adopt the Muslim way of life, wearing long dresses and a head scarf, submitting to her husband in all things. She knew she could never be a subservient wife. She planned to continue her career after marriage, and she planned to have children who would be free to live however they chose, not constricted by parental expectations or restrictions. Her heart was full when she realized that Ravi had not even imagined that kind of life for her. They were, she concluded, very much in tune with each other. And to become a doctor! With those beautiful, sensitive hands, those long, slender fingers, he could be a marvelous surgeon. It simply did not cross her mind that he might meet with prejudice when seeking admission to medical school. To her, he was perfection in every way—who could possibly think otherwise? Love, as is well known, can be blind.

In her next letter, Susan wrote of the religious question. "Are you a Muslim like your parents?" she asked him. "Will you expect me to convert?"

His reply was prompt and firm. "Although I was schooled in Muslim teachings I have not adopted that faith, to my parents' great disappointment. To be frank, I am not at all sure how I feel about the whole question of religion and religious faith. I yield to you on that score."

She wrote back: "Neither am I religious. My parents took me to a Baptist Sunday school once in a while, but it didn't take. I expect we will have many conversations about it someday, especially after we have children." That comment brought an end to the discussion for the time being.

Letters and postcards flowed back and forth between both sets of lovers; soon enough, Owen was signing off with "Love, Owen." Lois did the same. Susan and Ravi were less effusive, but love permeated their correspondence all the same.

One day Lois came bouncing in the front door, her face full of excitement and joy. "He's coming! Owen is coming!" she cried.

"Here? He's coming here? When? Why?"

"He found a neighbor to manage the farm for a week and decided to take a road trip. He said he was inspired by us. If we could take a vacation, so could he. So he is driving to Denver in his Model T and will stay with a relative who lives in Aurora."

"Yes, but when will he be here?"

"He said next week, probably Wednesday. He can stay for three days, then he has to get home again."

Susan was bowled over by such a gesture on Owen's part. In all their recent correspondence, Ravi had never mentioned coming to visit her. She reassured herself that he was probably having difficulty breaking away from his formidable mother. But it was Lois who deserved her attention just now.

"Lord have mercy, as my mother used to say, we'd better get cracking then."

"To do what?"

"Get this place shipshape, of course. Get you gussied up. You need a hair trim and probably a new outfit—maybe you can get some fabric from the store and get a new dress made. And certainly you need a new hat."

Lois was greatly amused by Susan's enthusiasm over her appearance; Susan never seemed to pay much attention to how she herself looked. Oh, she was tidy and clean, she kept her hair carefully bobbed, and she never wore mismatched colors or patterns, but all in all she was no fashion plate. Still, Lois had to agree that a few new items were overdue, and Owen's visit was a good excuse to indulge herself and Susan. As they had amicably agreed before the trip, Susan was paying back her share of the trip expenses, a small amount with every paycheck (she had kept meticulous records while they were traveling), so Lois once again had some money set aside.

"I want to get all our photos into an album too," Lois announced the next evening. They had all been developed, small black and white reminders of sights they had seen on the trip, but they still sat in a shoebox awaiting organization. "I'll get an album since it's your camera," Susan announced. The next day she bought a handsome leather-bound album at the five and ten cent store, its blank black pages ready for the photos, some tabs to secure the pictures, and white ink markers to identify what they were. Susan had a gift for organizing and a neat hand, so she undertook to sort the pictures, place them in the album and pen a notation under each one. What fun it was to relive the trip, day by day. Many of the pictures led to reminiscent conversations. Lois colored a few of the photos meticulously.

The Tuesday before Owen was to come was Election Day. Susan never missed a chance to vote; she was 20 when women gained the vote in America, and it was a privilege she never took lightly. Lois felt the same. They went to the voting site right after work, not even pausing for anything to eat, and waited quite some time before getting their ballots. Franklin Delano Roosevelt was indeed the Democratic candidate, as expected, running against the incumbent, Herbert Hoover. Most people they knew felt Hoover had done nothing to alleviate the misery in the country or to ease the Depression. He had spoken of "a chicken in every pot" but nothing occurred to make that a reality. Roosevelt represented hope, a change for the better. They devoutly hoped he would win. In the morning, they were delighted to learn that he had. Maybe things would get better. They were gratified, too, to wake up to clear, cold weather, with no sign of snow on the horizon. Lois had fretted about that possibility.

Wednesday was devoted to a flurry of expectation, tidying up the apartment, watching the weather and crossing their fingers that it wouldn't snow— Lois peered out the door every few minutes, just to be sure—and fussing over the meal they had prepared for him: Susan's mother's favorite meat loaf, fluffy mashed potatoes, canned green beans with crumbled bacon, and pumpkin pie for dessert. They knew they could never compete with Aunt Frances, but they were satisfied that the food was presentable and edible. They would put the meat loaf in the oven when he arrived and serve him pieces of toasted bread with egg salad on top for an appetizer, along with a glass of purloined wine, the bottle obtained somehow, somewhere by Lois over the weekend. She assured Susan that it was good quality wine, imported, not bathtub booze—they both knew of people had died from home-brewed liquor of various kinds. Susan didn't question Lois's acquisition or its source. Lois knew all kinds of people.

161

Owen came to the door with a bouquet of chrysanthemums in his hand. Welcomed into the apartment, he walked in tentatively, his fedora in his other hand. Susan was taken aback by his appearance; they had only seen him in farmers' overalls with a checkered shirt and a straw hat. Owen in a tailored suit, white shirt, plaid bow tie and a fedora gave the impression of a different man altogether. After she recovered her composure and managed not to let her astonishment show, she said she was just about to take Teddy for a walk and would be back in an hour or so.

Susan had given Owen the moments he needed in order to set the bouquet aside, get down on one knee and ask Lois to marry him. Lois never had a second's doubt; of course she would. She had known that he was the man she wanted to marry from the day they met. She quite forgot to put the meat loaf in the oven, start the potatoes, and open the can of beans. When Susan and Teddy returned and learned the joyous news, all three had a good laugh about the abandoned meal and went to a nearby Italian restaurant to celebrate, splurging on a large shared bowl of spaghetti and perfectly toasted garlic bread. Owen paid the bill. They went back to the apartment then and concluded the celebration with slices of the pumpkin pie Susan had made the day before.

Caught up in the romance of their love, Lois and Owen had not yet talked about what would happen after they married. Susan worried that her friend might move to Owen's farm, but she hesitated to ask. Then she had her own future to think about, for two weeks after Owen's romantic proposal came a missive from Ravi. Not taking the same approach as Owen, he sent Susan a poem on a postcard. It read, "I am getting down/On bended knee/I'm asking you/to marry me." To which Susan replied, jauntily, "You have pled your case/ With fervency/I do accept/so joyously." Not the best poetry she'd ever composed by any means (not that she'd composed much poetry except as a dreamy teenager), but it conveyed her sentiments perfectly well.

Both couples knew what issues lay before them. Lois was adamant that she would not move out of Colorado. Nor would Susan, who did not even want to leave Denver. With the experience in his parents' store, Ravi might be able to get a job as a clerk while awaiting entrance to medical school; she would continue at the library. Affording medical school was a grave concern, but Susan felt deep in her heart that somehow something would make it possible. A good many letters kept the postmen busy within which, with the best of intentions on all sides, the differences were addressed. Both women were determined that all the kinks be worked out before the marriages. (Of course, that was not possible; in marriage as in life, unanticipated kinks come along all the time; they could only address the hurdles that must be surmounted before their lives together could begin.)

To Lois's everlasting relief and gratitude, Owen declared—without any prompting on her part—that he would sell the farm in Illinois and buy one in Eastern Colorado if Lois would agree to become a farmer's wife. She knew that farming was where his heart lay; despite the harsh conditions they would face, she readily agreed to the compromise. She could always drive to Denver to get some city air.

Ravi had told Susan from the beginning that he did not want to run the store, and that he intended to move to Denver and seek entrance to the University of Colorado Medical School. His parents, he informed her, were not taking the news well and would not attend the wedding. Not only was he abandoning them; he was also abandoning their faith, for they had never given up their vision that he would convert. Their hearts were broken, but their son did not waver in his determination. Ravi and Susan would take over the apartment she and Lois had shared; it was conveniently within walking distance to work and to school and would be affordable on their combined salaries (Susan blithely assuming her new husband would have no trouble finding a job...).

It would of course be a double wedding. When and where were the first big decisions. Early spring was best, they all agreed—before planting time. Where to have it? Ravi was raised a Muslim even though he had not taken to it, Owen a Methodist; neither had a preference about where the wedding would be except, Ravi specified,

163

not in a Catholic church. Nor was either groom concerned about the form of the ceremony. Religion had not played a role in the upbringing of either Susan or Lois, but both wanted—for reasons they could not articulate—a church wedding. Some queries among friends led them to the Unitarian church on Lafayette Street, a gracious 19th-century stone building that suited them both nicely, with its large sanctuary and rich-voiced organ. Fortunately, the minister was amenable to performing a ceremony only superficially religious, more like a civil ceremony. The word "obey" was stricken from the wedding vows. Those matters settled, they turned to other considerations.

Although ordering printed invitations was a bit expensive, "We will only get married once," Lois declared. She created the design and in due time invitations went out. The guest list was not large—Susan's work colleagues (minus The Boss), a few special library patrons who had become friends, Enrico and Maria and some neighbors from her childhood, Lois's friends from the store and a few others she had made in her wilder days (but not the wildest ones), her father, and her brother Stanley and his wife, Maureen. (A duty invitation had also gone to George, who had snubbed her so blatantly at the funeral, but she did not anticipate a response. Lois did not expect her brother or her father to accept, though they might respond to the invitation.) They also sent invitations to everyone who had befriended them on the road trip, not supposing any of them would be able to come but just to let them know they were not forgotten. Never forgotten.

Lois was surprised and touched when Stanley RSVP'd that they would come to the wedding. He even offered to give the bride away, foreshadowing what his stiff-necked father would probably do in choosing not to walk his daughter down the aisle. He and Maureen would stay at the Oxford Hotel, he said, and they would finance a reception at the church after the ceremony. Neither bride had even imagined affording a reception; they had instead planned a quiet lunch at a nearby restaurant with just the wedding party. Lois accepted the offer, though, on the grounds that Stanley had not been much of a big brother to her when they were growing up. In fact, both her brothers had teased her mercilessly about her clumsiness—a factor, she always thought, of its following her into adulthood (although Susan insisted Lois was not any clumsier than anyone else, left-handed or not) and her height.

Lois had harbored a slight hope her father might walk her down the aisle, but he had declined, not even nicely. He made clear that he was disappointed in her choice of a husband. Couldn't she do better than a farmer, for god's sake? At which point tempers flared on both sides; Lois doubted her father would make an appearance at all. Rather than being disappointed she felt numb, and grateful that her brother would do the honors for her.

Miss T. Young and the dressmaker were invited to be the brides' attendants. Each groom asked a special friend—Ravi, knowing his father would not come, asked his "almost brother" Clarence Snow, a near neighbor in Hallelujah! who had been a close friend of his for years and had, he told Susan, helped him keep his sanity, while Owen asked Rupert Browning, a colleague from the school where he had once taught. Enrico would escort Susan down the aisle. Susan would go first, then Lois. The men would not be "giving away" the brides but rendering them into the matrimonial love and care of their soon-to-be husbands.

It was to be a simple occasion, with minimal fuss and expense. The brides' attendants could wear favorite frocks. The men need not get tuxedos, just wear nice suits, and their best men the same. For Lois, Owen had his mother's wedding ring re-sized, while Ravi and Susan picked out a plain gold band, not costly but just right for her. When it came to wedding dresses, though, all bets were off. The brides had agreed to choose gowns as frugally as possible, but still they must be memorable and bring out the best in each woman. Bit by bit, Lois was able to bring home swatches of satin and lace from the store's tailor-made department, enough for two gowns.

The gowns Lois designed were stunning. Ankle length, Lois's had a shirred, fitted bodice with a square neckline. At the waist, the gown flared around her full figure. Her cuffs and neckline were trimmed with lace. In her hair she wore a small white cap decorated with lace lilies of the valley. Gloria's pearls adorned her throat. Susan's gown was empire style, calf length, with a rounded neckline and three-quarter sleeves. Here and there were touches of lace. In her hair she wore a band of crocheted daisies, a wedding gift from Maria. Offered Lois's turquoise necklace, she declined, preferring instead a small pendant with a silhouette of a Victorian woman's face, hanging from a black ribbon, which had belonged to her grandmother and her mother. Neither wanted to wear a veil. They both went to a professional photographer to have portraits taken in their finery. Each would carry a small nosegay of daffodils, since they were in season and could be gathered from the park behind their old apartment; Miss T. Young took on that last-minute task and tied the bouquets expertly.

Both brides splurged on new shoes, ivory satin-covered low heels, the traditional "something new" that would probably never be worn again. But after all, one only got married once, they told each other. And Lois did get a reasonable discount at the department store. In a bow to tradition, they covered "something old" with the jewelry; "something borrowed" became, for Lois, the hairpins belonging to Susan that secured her hat, and for Susan a pair of gloves loaned to her by Miss T. Young. "Something blue" was a little more challenging; they decided that the ribbons on the bouquets would do the trick.

Of course it was sorrowful for Ravi that his parents boycotted his wedding, and to Lois that her father did the same. Susan missed her father acutely that day. But they all determined it would be a joyous occasion despite the absences, and indeed it was. Stanley and Maureen came the day before the wedding and treated the two couples to dinner at the hotel. (George had not only chosen to disregard the invitation, he also did not send congratulations or a gift.)

Gifts began arriving: two wedding quilts from Ida, vases and platters and cross-stitched wall hangings "(Home Sweet Home" on one and "God Bless This House" on another. Should the givers ever arrive for a visit, they would hang up the stitchings while the guests were present). One of Lois's friends sent a china teapot, and one of

Susan's farm neighbors sent a large box of canned plum preserves. Susan knew that sending the parcel must have been expensive, and she promptly sent back a note of profuse thanks. She would of course share the preserves with Lois. Each of the couples received some gilded picture frames; Lois and Owen got a silver serving spoon. It was great fun to open the gifts and thank the givers.

    Stanley and his wife arrived two days before the wedding after a long, tiring train trip from Boston and invited Lois and Susan to dinner at their hotel. Stanley apologized to his sister. He said he regretted not keeping in touch and promised to do better. "I'd been feeling angry and bitter for such a long time," he told her. "She ruined my childhood. George and I didn't even have a real childhood. We just kept out of her way as much as we could. I'm so very sorry for the way we treated you; I hope you can forgive me one day. When I met Maureen, she helped me get past all my pent-up bad feelings and start a new life." With that little speech, he handed Lois an envelope. "It's not much," he said, "but it might help. Seems like the least I can do." Lois, who hardly ever cried, hugged her brother (who was taller than she by a couple of inches) and wiped her eyes. "Just your being here is the best gift I could ever have," she told him. She had never been one to hold or nurture grudges; forgiveness was much simpler than bitterness. ("Not much" turned out to be $500, a small fortune in those days and times. It helped the farm prosper.)

    To Susan, Stanley was something of a surprise. Having met Lois's father, a tall but stocky, square-jawed man with hair trimmed to the nth degree and bushy eyebrows, she was taken aback by his son, who was quite tall, slender, "Hollywood handsome" as they liked to say then, and as blonde as his father was dark-haired. "He takes after Gloria," Lois told her. "If she hadn't drunk herself to death, she would have been the most beautiful woman in any room full of people," a comment that had made both of them momentarily sad for what might have been. Maureen, a well-decked-out redhead who wore her clothes as a model would, with off-handed, unselfconscious grace, almost matched her husband in height. She too surprised Susan with her warmth and charm.

It fascinated Susan that Lois had never once spoken of Owen's being two inches shorter than she, and two years younger. (Ravi was in fact five years younger than Susan.) One of Lois's criteria for a husband had been that he would match her in height; Owen did not, and Lois appeared not to care one whit. He was her dream man in every other respect. What did a few inches matter? She wore low-heeled shoes but stood tall and straight as she always did. Susan was amused at the fates, that she and Ravi made a match when he would have been so perfect for Lois, being even taller than she. But such is life.

Although it was early April and could have been cold or rainy, the weather was agreeable on the chosen day in 1933. The air was crisp but not cold; the sky sparkled bright and blue; the sun shone down benignly. A slight breeze wafted through the air, and birds could be seen busily building nests. The ceremony went off without a hitch. The church organist, who had agreed on a fee of only $5 (gallantly paid by Stanley), played the wedding march and the triumphant traditional recessional as well as the two hymns that they had mutually chosen, "For the Beauty of the Earth" and "Come, Thou Fount of Every Blessing." The glorious sounds of the instrument filled the sanctuary and the hearts of those who heard it. It could not have been a more perfect start to the rest of their lives.

Between the two friends, attendance at the ceremony was larger than they had thought it would be, although the crowd hardly filled the large, beautiful sanctuary. Still, everyone who was there was a friend who, they knew, rejoiced in their happiness. Their hearts were full.

By letter and telephone Maureen had arranged a reception at the church—delicate hors d'oeuvres, fresh fruit, punch (nonalcoholic) and a variety of cookies. She even ordered a wedding cake, to the delight of the brides. Three tiers high, it had two bride-and-groom figures on top. Lois was so touched by it that she burst into tears, distressing Owen until she explained that they were happy tears. She and Stanley had a long way to go to truly become brother and sister, but it was an excellent start.

After the reception, cheered on their way with showers of rice, Lois and Owen headed Theda toward their new farm, where they honeymooned for three days while a neighbor cared for the stock. Owen was full of apologies for not being able to give his new wife a real honeymoon. She told him she could have used the gift from Stanley or sold a diamond ring to pay for it but she would rather they put the money toward their new life together. She did not care where they honeymooned, as long as they were together. Teddy went with them, then accompanied them back to Illinois after the honeymoon to help Aunt Frances settle into her new life in Springfield with her cousin Jeanine and to close the sale on the farm (Owen knew he had been lucky to find a buyer, a young man fresh out of college who was eager to start farming using the new methods being promoted and agreed to make monthly payments, sent directly to Owen. Distrust of banks still ran deep) and, after all that, to start their married life on the Eastern Colorado farm.

Owen had intended to bring his dog back to the new farm with him, but Aunt Frances had become very attached to the animal after Owen sold the farm and declared she wanted to keep the dog with her. Owen arranged for the beautiful German Shepherd to be spayed so she would not have any more puppies and lovingly bade her adieu, knowing she would have a good home with his aunt and his cousin.

Parting with Teddy had hurt Susan sorely, but she knew it was for the best, for Ravi and she would live in the city while he applied to medical school and did what he could to earn money in the meantime. Neither would be home much to take the little dog for walks or to give him the attention he needed and deserved; he was better off at the farm where he could run free and chase whatever needed chasing. Susan vowed to come and see him as soon as she could; she sobbed for hours after the newlyweds and their canine companion had departed. Ravi waited her out patiently, patting her shoulder from time to time and holding her close. His reassurance, when he might easily have been doing something else, told Susan once again

169

how right her choice of a life partner had been.

It was several days later, after a rapturous honeymoon at a rustic resort in the Rockies (financed by the sale of one of Gloria's diamonds, Lois's wedding gift to them; Susan gave the Andertons a framed photograph of the two of them together in the park, taken with Lois's camera by a passerby one fine day and colored by an artist friend who frequented the library), before Susan had time to write in her journal again. They had been back in the apartment in Capitol Hill, setting things to rights, a couple of days before she found time to sit down and try to recapture the events of the last week.

Life seems like a fairy tale. Ravi is such a tender, thoughtful lover, such a kind, generous man—how did I ever get so lucky? If I were religious, I would say I have been blessed. Awhile ago I told L that our road trip was so bizarre, with such unimaginable outcomes, that I ought to write a book about it. She laughed until tears ran down her cheeks. When she had recovered she said, "Sure, you could write a book, but who in the world would believe it?"

Epilogue

Gradually, times got better. The Roosevelt Administration put millions of people back to work, and the nation perked up its head and started, incrementally, to hope again. The New Deal began having an observable impact on the economy. Years later the travelers would learn that the year of their trip was by far the worst one of the Great Depression. Tensions slowly eased as time went by, and indeed the worst seemed to be over by the time Franklin Delano Roosevelt was reelected in 1936.

Thankfully, both Ravi and Owen were considered to be in essential occupations and were not drafted when war came yet again, although they both fell within the upper end of the age limits. Privately, Susan and Lois shared their relief, mingled with some guilt, for so many women lost husbands, brothers and sons during that trying time. Both friends put their whole hearts into the war effort on the home front, learning to cook without sugar, collecting newspapers for Boy Scout drives, smashing tin cans and turning them in for scrap, coming up with a dozen creative ways to serve hamburger, growing victory gardens, volunteering with the Red Cross (Susan) and helping out at neighbors' farms at harvest time, with the young men away at war (Lois). They were mightily relieved when the war finally ended and devastated when President Roosevelt died just before VE day in Paris.

Susan and Lois kept their friendship intact. They regularly exchanged letters, shared family holidays, talked on the telephone (when Lois could get a free line), and visited each other as often as they could. No sisters could have been closer. Of course, all was not sweetness and light. Over the years, there were heart aches and heart breaks, disappointments and failures, anxieties and anguish. Not every day shimmered with delight; not every decision worked out as hoped. Still, the two women who had forged an unbreakable bond while on the road to adventure held each other up through every trauma, soothed hurt feelings, maneuvered their way through the mazes of parenthood and experienced the exigencies of aging together. They had chosen their mates wisely, too, for the marriages were solid and rewarding even when the road got bumpy—which it did, quite naturally, from time to time.

Miraculously, Ravi was admitted to the medical school, where he excelled as his wife had known he would. Though she never told her husband, Susan privately attributed his admission to her long-enduring friendship with a library patron who often came to the library not knowing what he sought; she would always manage to find just the right book for the mood he was in. Turned out he was the admissions director at the medical school, something Susan had never known about him. One day as they were chatting, she happened to mention that her husband, who was clerking at a hardware store (having, to their great relief, found a job within days of their return to Denver and having had years of experience as a clerk), had hopes of becoming a doctor. Learning that a recent application from one Ravi Crandall had in fact come from his favorite librarian's spouse caused the patron to smooth out the admission process; Ravi was in. With admission came a full-tuition scholarship which Ravi didn't remember applying for and the source of which neither of the Crandalls ever knew—although Susan suspected the same man. He would never acknowledge his generosity, but he made a point of being present when Ravi graduated and personally congratulating him, and Susan suspected that he influenced Ravi's getting an internship at Denver General Hospital instead of somewhere farther away.

Ravi inevitably met with prejudice in medical school, as did the sole woman student, but he overcame hostility with his quiet ways, refusing to be baited, and with his remarkable skills. Those long fingers she had noticed when they first met served him well in the operating room; he became an acclaimed and sought-after surgeon, specializing in plastic surgery after so many veterans returned from combat disfigured in some way. Susan marveled at Ravi's magic with restoring faces. Before and after photos left her awed and amazed.

Ravi's parents never forgave him and showed no interest in meeting their grandchildren—born not long after their marriage, for Susan was anxious to have children before she got too old.

Amid producing a family of three satisfactorily average-height children (neither conspicuously tall nor shorter than average), Susan, the country girl now thoroughly attuned to city life, continued her work at the library and became its director after The Boss keeled over at his desk one day, gone without even letting out one final roar. Susan loved her work. She relished re-creating the little county library, introducing a special children's section and starting weekly story time, when she or a volunteer read to the children. (Many a time, Susan's own children sat on her lap while she read a story.) She updated the system of purchasing books, making sure the latest best sellers (even if they were a little racy or poorly written as was sometimes the case) were displayed prominently on a separate shelf, and did away with punitive fines for overdue books. A nickel a day was exorbitant, she had always thought, so the fine became a penny a day, forgiven if the book was returned within three days. She overhauled the cataloguing process, trusting her employees to make correct entries. She loved seeing children bounce happily into the library, head for the children's section, and eagerly choose their next books to take home. She made sure the clerks were always cheerful, greeting patrons with a smile. Her library was a happy place.

Susan had to work at motherhood. Much as she had longed for it, she found it challenging beyond anything she might have envisioned. Domesticity did not come naturally to her, a trait perhaps exacerbated by her years of toil at the farm. Still, she gave everything she could to her girls: unstinting love and support, an always-available ear for listening, respect and encouragement. Among her friends who were parents she was a heretic, for she hired nannies to care for her little ones and went right on working, sent them to preschool and kindergarten, and pursued her career. She made sure her daughters knew how to cook and sew and such (with considerable help from Lois, who also delighted in creating the latest fashions for them), but most of all she instilled in them all her deep, abiding love of books. Time with her children was most often spent reading or talking about books.

On more than one occasion she had to do battle to save her little facility; growth and budgets threatened to swallow it up into the larger metropolitan library system. But Susan was not entering the fray unarmed—battalions of parents and patrons spoke up for her library, with its convenient location, excellent services and caring staff. Eventually the county library was absorbed into the city system anyway, but it became a safely ensconced branch library, which was fine with Susan.

She even started a bookmobile, locating a retired school bus that was about to be scrapped and persuading a friend, one of her loyal patrons, to repair it, spruce it up, and install bookshelves. Once word got out, book donations began pouring in; soon, there were enough to fill all the shelves. Volunteers took turns driving the bus into the countryside. Susan went along a time or two, thrilled to see children running toward the bus when they saw it coming, crowding inside to pick out books, and conscientiously returning books they had checked out. One volunteer, an older woman whose children had left home and failed to provide her with grandchildren nearby, began a weekly story hour. Susan's heart was full.

She and Ravi encouraged their daughters to follow their dreams, whatever they might be. "Women can become whatever they dream of being," she often told them. Her daughters would go to college, explore their country and the world, and follow their passions once they had discovered what those passions were. In the later years of her long life, she saw her belief in women's coming into their own gradually become reality.

And yes, Ravi and Susan eventually got a dog of their very own, "For the children," Susan said, but in her heart she knew it was really for her. They named him Franklin, after the president, and called him Frankie. He was small, like Teddy, and cuddly, a loving fur ball who had been abandoned at the city pound and needed a home. With the exception of Teddy, no dog was ever loved more. No dog was ever more patient either, submitting to being hauled around in a wagon, dressed up in frilly clothes, and rocked like a baby.

As for Teddy, he was succeeded by other dogs, but there would never be another Teddy. After he died, having lived an amazing 18 years with the Andertons (and who knows how old he was when they found him?), Lois found an old photograph, taken on the trip, of Susan holding the little dog. She carefully colored it, put it into a silver frame and sent it to Susan, who wept copiously when it came and hung it over the mantel piece (for by then, thanks to Ravi's achievements as a noted surgeon, they owned a comfortable house just off University Boulevard which had, to her delight, a fireplace). At long last, they also got a private telephone line; it took a little longer for Lois and Owen to get one.

Lois, the city girl, became the quintessential farmer's wife, mastering all the attendant tasks and becoming a renowned cook. She learned to milk cows and feed chickens, to collect eggs and to humanely butcher hens too old to lay any longer. She canned fruits and vegetables and made preserves, planted a large vegetable garden, and grew roses. She went out into the fields with her husband when he plowed and planted. She loved it all, even the inevitable ups and downs of a farmer's life. In time, the farmyard symphony, sometimes accentuated with a coyote's howls, could lure her to sleep.

As she had years before promised herself, she became the mother she had always longed to have. She gave birth quickly and joyously, nursed and cuddled her babies, read to her children and tucked them in every night, wept when they went off to school then became immersed in PTA, 4-H and county fairs, praised them fulsomely when they deserved it and mastered a look of profound disappointment when they fell short (far more effective than any conceivable punishment), comforted them through childish hurt feelings and scraped knees, played games with them, taught them both all of domestic arts, and loved them wholly, unconditionally. Neither one ever left the house or returned to it without a hug and a kiss on the forehead. Neither one ever had a moment's doubt that their mother loved them, no matter what. Lois held her breath when her son was drafted for the Korean War and breathed a sigh of relief when he was sent not overseas but to Texas to train mechanics, for he had inherited his father's gift with machinery. Thus she and Owen sent their offspring off into the world confident, capable and clear-eyed, eager to discover their own passions just as their parents had found theirs — for each other and for their innate interests.

Once in a while, Lois was struck with a moment of sadness that her mother had missed out on such joy and fulfilment and that her father had become so completely estranged, clinging to his outdated views even as the world changed around him, but these visitations seldom lasted long, and in the end only engendered continued efforts to be the exact opposite of her parents. She was not able to mourn when her father died and felt no guilt for her lack of grief. Characteristically, he left her only a small legacy — his ancient Rolls Royce, for which she and Owen had no use whatsoever. (The antique car did, however, bring a tidy sum when they sold it.)

The artistic pieces of her soul were fed by discovering the quiet pleasure of quilting; she knew she could never match Ida's skill, but she made some county-fair-prize winning quilts all the same. As for the supposed clumsiness that had haunted her childhood, it completely vanished; Owen had often told her it had been all in her head, thanks to her brothers' teasing. She decided he had probably been right, for her hands became as nimble as could be, left-handed or not.

And she did nourish her relationship with Stanley, although she and George never found common ground. (Lois was the first to admit she didn't try very hard; one letter to George that went unanswered was enough for her.) Stanley and Maureen did not have children of their own, so they doted on the two Anderton offspring, sending gifts and cards, always remembering Christmases and birthdays. On one memorable occasion, they even took the children to Washington, D.C., to see the sights.

She and Owen had two children, one boy, one girl, one taller than average, one just average, who grew up to lead happy, prosperous lives (though only one took up farming; the other became an art and music teacher) and in due time provided them with grandchildren, who, when they came to visit, were plied with homemade goodies. Their favorite was oatmeal raisin. "They're good for you," Lois would tell them with a smile. The youngsters didn't care about that; the point was that they were yummy. The Andertons stayed on the farm well past the time they were able to work the land and care for the animals, so they leased the land to a tenant farmer and sold the livestock in order to keep the farm going.

Eventually they gave in, deeded the farm to their daughter and moved to Denver, near Susan and Ravi. The Crandall brood—three beautiful, lightly bronze-skinned daughters—all found satisfying careers at a time when doors were slowly beginning to open for women. The oldest, to Ravi's great pleasure, chose to become a doctor like her father, a family physician rather than a surgeon. She joined a practice in Chicago (of all places!), where the underprivileged were treated along with paying patients, after spending some time in Africa volunteering at free clinics where she vaccinated children against various terrible diseases.

Their middle daughter became a college professor, teaching English as Susan had once dreamed of doing and regularly publishing erudite treatises in distinguished periodicals, and the "baby of the family" became a moderately successful writer of police procedurals. Susan was duly impressed that her child could come up with such intricate puzzles and create a detective (a woman, of course) whom readers followed from book to book. She basked in the success of all three of her daughters and gave thanks to whatever gods may be that they had so many opportunities unavailable to her own generation. Only one of them provided her with grandchildren to dote on, but that was fine with her. Her daughters were fulfilled and happy; that was all that mattered.

Life for the two kindred spirits was rich to the end. Both outlived their husbands and, to the surprise of no one in either family, moved into a suburban townhouse to live out their lives together after they were widowed. "Like Marilla and her friend in *Anne of Green Gables*," Susan wryly remarked, to which Lois responded, "I haven't read that one. What's it about?" eliciting a loving smile from Susan.

Oh, yes, and "Pop 121.5": Ravi explained that the half a person was actually a much loved pet, a loyal sheepdog which one resident had lobbied to be memorialized. The other 120 residents had complied, for the dog's owner was the mayor of the little town. (Or, perhaps the dog had been the mayor...) The population of the town, sadly, declined until one day there was almost no one left, and the Crandalls closed their store and moved to Wichita. Ravi learned of their departure from his erstwhile best man, who had also left Hallelujah! Kansas for greener fields, so to speak, but kept up with happenings there, knowing how sad Ravi was about being estranged from his stubborn parents and wanting his friend to at least know where they were and what they were doing.

The Batsons and other friends they had made along the road were, as promised, never forgotten. Long before the wedding sent the friends down separate paths, Judy got her doll, a porcelain beauty with golden hair, arms and legs that moved and blue eyes that blinked. Bend her at the waist and she said "Mama" in a sweet, small voice. Susan had found the doll for fifty cents (wardrobe included; what a bargain) at a sad little bankruptcy sale one Saturday while walking Teddy. The two friends were confident Judy would take very good care of her doll. They wrapped her thickly in newspaper to be sure she didn't get broken en route and were pleased when Judy's mother sent a letter thanking them for the gift, which had arrived intact. Until she grew up, Judy got a birthday card and a gift every year from both Lois and Susan. After she was grown, Judy came to Colorado to meet her two benefactors and entwined herself, to the satisfaction of everyone involved, into their lives. "She's a real talker," Susan commented one day. "She must have been saving up all those words for later," Lois replied with a chuckle.

Caleb and Martha Schmidt were the recipients of a framed photograph of their barn, intricately colored by Lois. Ida Hornby received a vividly colorful bolt of fabric and a framed picture of the quilt in the general store—the photo had come out well after all. Lois colorized it beautifully from memory. The two friends were thanked and informed that the photograph had pride of place in the Hornby parlor. They did, eventually, hear from the Dawsons. Reginald had found a job in St. Louis though not at the botanical gardens right away (he worked at a flower shop until he finally got hired at the gardens). Little Susan got a birthday card and a check every year from each of them, and they vowed to visit St. Louis someday to meet the miracle baby. And one day they did, to the delight of all concerned. By then Susan Dawson had a little sister, named, to their surprise and pleasure, Lois. The families exchanged their year's news every Christmas, never losing touch. Thus Susan and Lois learned that Reginald had registered for the draft right after Pearl Harbor but been rejected for weak eyesight, and that Little Susan had grown a prize-winning pumpkin. It is with such small tidbits that friendships are cemented.

And what of Theda?

She stayed with the Andertons, patiently taking them where they needed to go until the family grew and required a roomier, fully enclosed vehicle. Owen had left his Model T with the farm he sold—thanks to his years under the hood of that one he was adept at keeping Theda running for a few more years, but after having a child they needed a different kind of conveyance, so they retired Theda and bought a sturdy sedan. Theda was put out to pasture, sheltered somewhat by the barn overhang, where she served variously as a club house, a fortress, a fox family's den, a robbers' roost (magpies storing their treasures there), and a home for assorted small creatures. Several generations of barn cats came into the world on her seats. Bombarded daily by the sun in summer, battered by wind and weather year round, she endured all, aging slowly and uncomplainingly as the years went by. Hail eventually caved in her roof. Mice set up housekeeping in her engine. Engine parts, stiffened by lack of use, adhered to each other. Once, she was even struck by lightning, leaving a jagged hole in one side. Her once almost-new tires fell to pieces and the wheels sank into the ground.

But when the Andertons' son wanted to take her apart and turn in the metal for scrap during World War II, Lois adamantly refused. Theda would not end her days that way, providing metal that would be used to make ammunition to kill people in yet another war. Not a chance.

After a good many years, Theda gave in to the ravages of time and the elements and collapsed in a heap. Suffused with guilt for not having tended better to her former companion (though she had been extraordinarily busy for years and simply had not found the time or energy), Lois acted to preserve what remained. She arranged the bedraggled heap into the shape of a headstone, welded the pieces together (another farming skill she had mastered), and had these words engraved:

"Theda, faithful chariot, took two friends on a trip that changed their lives forever. Rest in peace."

Thus did what survived of the tough old flivver become a fitting memorial to friendship, adventure, daring, and love.

Made in the USA
Lexington, KY
24 October 2019